Fundamental
Affair

C. L. Conolly

FUNDAMENTAL AFFAIR

KILLER WORDS PUBLISHING
Copyright © 2020 by C. L. Conolly
Cover model is Zella Sebesta
Cover photo by EPiC
Author Photo by Julie Moore Photography

C. L. Conolly
www.clconolly.com
clconolly@gmail.com
New Ulm, Texas

ISBN-13: 978-0-9886876-3-9

Printed in the United States of America

10 9 8 7 6 5 4 3 2 1

My name is Mackenzie Leigh. I wasn't born with that name; it was a name I chose after my mother abandoned me. I never knew my father and my mother threw me away like garbage. This is my story.

Also written by C. L. Conolly

<u>Lone Titles</u>
Friendly Misfortunes

<u>Affair Series</u>
Forbidden Affair
Family Affair

Fundamental Affair

One

I was born to a single mother. She always treated me as though I was a burden on her, I wasn't even sure if she ever actually loved me. For as long as I could remember, she would drop me off at the neighbor's house first thing in the morning and leave me there until well after dinner.

I began calling the neighbor Auntie May around the time that I was two. Some days I wasn't even dressed yet when my mother would take me over there. Auntie May would just dress me in one of the outfits that no longer fit each of her girls, Diamond and Jade.

Every year on my birthday my mother would rush me out of the house as soon as I woke up and insist I go next door. Life was normal, well normal for me, up until I was six.

On my sixth birthday, my mother came rushing into my room and pulled my blanket off the bed. I was startled awake and sat up, disoriented.

"Get out, now," she yelled.

As soon as I realized what was going on, I jumped up out of the bed and ran out the front door, headed to Auntie May's house. I reached the front door and lifted my hand to press the button for the doorbell, when the door swung open. Auntie May along with Diamond and

Jade stood on the other side with a homemade cupcake in her hand. There was a number six candle on top already lit up.

"Happy birthday," the three of them said emphatically.

I was startled, but I still laughed.

"Make a wish and blow out your candle," Auntie May told me.

Every year I would wish for the same thing, for my mother to spend a day with me. I closed my eyes, made the wish and blew out the candle. A couple of months after my birthday, I thought my wish had finally come true.

The day started pretty normal. I woke up, washed my hands and face, along with brushing my teeth before getting dressed to head over to Auntie May's house. Trying to be as quiet as possible, so as not to disturb my mother, I headed out to the living room. Reaching the front door, I sat down in the foyer in order to put my shoes on.

"You wanna do something fun today?" my mother asked me, after I had my shoes tied.

"Sure," I said, unsure of what she meant.

"Go brush your hair and meet me back here so we can go."

"Where are we going?"

"It's a surprise. Now go," she said.

I smiled my biggest smile at her and nodded emphatically. Being so excited that she wanted to spend time with me, I ran off to brush my hair, then hurried back out to the living room. When I saw my mother waiting for me by the front door, I felt as though my birthday wish had finally come true. She grabbed my hand and led me out to the car.

"Good morning Kenzie, Bec. Where are you headed off to today?" May asked, as she sat on her front porch.

"I just thought I would spend the day with my daughter," my mother told her, as she loaded me into the car.

"Have fun," May said, waving at me with a worried smile on her face.

I waved back and touched my shoulders then poked my cheeks, flashing her our secret hand signal to let her know I was happy and she did the same back. May had come up with secret hand signals for us so she would know how I was feeling. She said it was a way for me to understand and express my feelings, even if I didn't want to, or couldn't, talk about it.

I watched my mother peer at me through the rear view mirror with a look on her face that looked as though she was trying to figure out where to take me. I didn't know what she had planned, but I was just imagining we were going on a vacation for the day.

She pulled up to a building with probably twenty floors and parked the car. After she climbed out of the front seat, she closed her door and leaned against it, smoking a cigarette. My mother looked around the parking lot, seeming nervous, before she flicked the cigarette as far as she could and opened the back door, in order to help me out of the car.

"What are we going to do here?" I asked her, as she led me inside the building and over to the elevator.

Without saying a word, she pressed the call button to go up and we waited for the doors to open.

When the tone sounded to signal it had arrived, we both stepped in. My mother kept her hand against the open doors, in order to make sure they didn't close. Tears formed in my eyes as she reached up and pressed the button for the top floor. Without a single word, she stepped out of the elevator. As the elevator doors closed, separating us, she just stood there motionless, glaring at me.

I thought to myself, *'maybe she is playing hide and seek. I bet I am supposed to find her when the elevator gets back to the bottom'*. As the elevator approached the top floor, I pressed my back against the far wall as the doors opened. At the top, a gentleman entered the elevator and looked down at me as he pressed the button for the lobby.

I slowly slid down into a sitting position, wedging myself into the corner. I pulled my knees up to my chest when the elevator started to move. He eventually spoke to me.

"Are you lost?" he asked.

"No, my mother and I are playing hide and seek. She sent me to the top to give her enough time to hide," I told him, no longer believing my own story and tears began to form in my eyes.

"Hmm," the man grunted, as he rode the elevator down to the lobby.

When the elevator arrived and the doors opened, the man turned back toward me, still huddled in the corner. He placed his hand over the doors in order to hold them open.

"Good luck. I hope you find your mother," he said, helping me to my feet and holding the doors open, giving me the chance to exit the elevator first.

I smiled at him and watched as he exited the building. I looked around the lobby and noticed a line of people at the front desk. I observed each person in line, just to see if one of them happened to be my mother. She wasn't there.

I stood in front of the closed elevator doors and noticed a seating area no one was occupying. I looked under the tables and behind the chairs knowing in the back of my mind, I wasn't really going to find her.

I wandered over to the side table between two over-sized arm chairs. I climbed under the table and there I waited, hoping my mother would find me.

It felt like hours before a woman with shoulder length, blonde hair, wearing a dress jacket and a pin on name tag that read Lorie, came over to talk to me.

"Hey there, are you lost?" she asked.

I nodded acknowledging her, but I didn't speak. She nodded back and extended her hand to help me come out from under the table.

"What's going on?" she asked, helping me up into one of the large arm chairs.

"My mommy brought me here to play hide and seek," I told her.

"Hide and seek, huh? Is she supposed to look for you, or are you supposed to look for her?"

"I'm 'posed to look for her, but I'm scared. I don't want to look alone. When I play at Auntie May's house, Jade hides with me, or Auntie May helps me find Jade and Diamond," I told her.

"And who are they?"

"They live next door. I usually spend all day with them, but today mommy said we were going to do something fun and she brought me here, but I'm not having any fun."

"Well, my name is Lorie. How about you sit here and wait to see if your mommy finds you. I'm just going to be right over at that desk. If you need anything, just wave and I'll come over, okay?" she said, pointing at the front desk where she was standing when I came out of the elevator.

I nodded and she patted me on my knee before heading back over to the big desk by the front doors. I watched her as she picked up the phone and called someone. She talked for a few moments, then hung up.

I stared at my shoes, waiting, hoping my mother would come out from wherever she was hiding and find me.

I sat in the chair, with my legs dangling, crying to myself. A couple of times someone came over and asked if I was okay. The first time, I pulled my legs up into the chair with me and laid against the back, ignoring the lady.

The second time, I turned my face into the back of the chair and grunted. When she walked away, I looked up and saw a police woman enter the building. The officer stepped up to the counter and spoke to Lorie. I watched as they conversed for a few moments, then Lorie pointed at me. I thought I was in trouble, so I climbed back under the table and hid.

While I was there, the police woman came over and sat down in one of the oversized chairs. At first, she didn't speak. She just sat there quietly, then all of a sudden, she spoke.

"You're not in trouble. I just want to talk," she said.

I poked my head out and she assisted me into the other oversized arm chair that I had occupied before.

"So, I hear you are playing hide and seek with your mommy," she said.

"Yes ma'am," I replied.

"Do you know what your mommy's name is?"

"No ma'am, but Auntie May calls her Bec."

"Well, what's your name?"

"I'm Mackenzie, but Auntie May calls me Kenzie," I told her.

"Who's Auntie May?" she asked.

"She lives next door."

"Okay. Do you know where you live?"

"In a house."

"Do you know a phone number I could call to talk to your mommy?"

"I know nine one one. That's only for emergencies, like if someone is hurt, or there is a fire, or a bad man is trying to come into the house."

"That's right. Nine one one is only for emergencies. Do you know how to contact your mommy?" she continued to question me.

"No, but Auntie May does," I told her.

"Do you know a phone number to contact Auntie May?"

"Nope, the only phone number I know is nine one one. I'm six."

"Okay Mackenzie, what is your last name?"

"I only had one name, Mackenzie. That was the last name I was called. I don't remember having any other names," I told her.

"Alright, you stay here and I'll be right back," the officer told me, before walking back over to the counter to talk to Lorie again.

After a few moments, she talked into her radio that was clipped to her shoulder, then headed back over to where I was sitting.

"Okay Mackenzie, I'm Officer Leigh and I'm going to need you to come with me," she said, in an official police tone.

"Am I in trouble?" I asked, as I started to cry.

"No sweetie, you're not in trouble. I just need you to come with me, so we can try to find your mommy."

I wiped the tears off my face and sniffed hard to pull the mucus back up my nose. I used the bottom of my shirt to clean my face, then walked with Officer Leigh out to her cop car.

"Bye Lorie," I said, as we walked out the door.

"Bye bye," she said, waving.

Officer Leigh placed me in the backseat of her patrol car and drove me to the police station. She asked me questions, while I was wondering what happened to my mother.

"Do you know why your mommy would leave you there at the hotel without supervision?" she asked.

"I don't know. Normally she takes me to Auntie May's house. I just thought my birthday wish had finally come true," I told the officer.

"What was your birthday wish?"

"I close my eyes, wish my mommy would spend just one day with me, then blow out the candle."

"That sounds like a great birthday wish," Officer Leigh said, as she pulled into the police station parking lot.

I watched through the car window, noticing a group of uniformed officers standing around outside. At six years old, I was terrified that I was in trouble. I cried quietly, as I thought I was going to jail for being out somewhere alone.

Officer Leigh parked her vehicle at the curb, in front of the police station and got out. I watched as she talked to a few other officers and pointed at me. Every one of them turned and looked at me, crying in the backseat, watching them through the window. I looked down at my hands and tried to figure out what had changed.

I didn't understand why this day was different than any other day. I was trying to understand why my mother didn't just let me go with Auntie May. I wanted to play with Jade and Diamond. I just wanted to go home.

I had closed my eyes and imagined what I would have been doing if I had made it to Auntie May's house, when the car door swung open, interrupting my thought. I opened my eyes and noticed a male officer standing outside, waiting for me to exit the vehicle.

"Come on, get out of the car," he said to me, presenting his hand to me.

I recoiled back into the car, away from him and pressed my back against the closed door on the other side of the car. I wasn't going to get out until I saw Officer Leigh, but he reached in, grabbed my leg and tried to pull me out when I refused to get out on my own.

"Let me go! No! Don't touch me!" I screamed at him, kicking my legs to get free, as he continued to pull on me to get me out of the car.

"It's okay, Bailey. I got this," I heard Officer Leigh say, getting between the male officer and me.

Once he let go and walked away, I stopped screaming. Officer Leigh peeked into the car at me and smiled.

"Don't worry Mackenzie, I won't let anyone hurt you," Leigh told me.

She helped me out of the car and I wrapped my arms around her leg. She started to walk, but with me adding an extra appendage, she was having difficulty. She reached down and lifted me into her arms, carrying me into the station. She placed me down at her feet when she checked in at the front desk. I huddled around her legs and waited for her to finish.

She took my hand and led me through the inner doors. As we walked passed about a dozen desks, the ones without anyone sitting in the chairs just had papers laid out on top, but the ones with officers occupying them were cleared and organized. I figured it was to give the impression that the slackers outside were busy working, when in actuality, they were just taking a break. Officer Leigh took me to a room that had a table and three chairs, with a mirror on one wall.

"Wait here, I'll be right back," she told me.

"No, don't leave me," I said, beginning to cry, loudly.

"I'm not leaving you. I just need to go make a phone call," she said, kneeling down in front of me.

"Can I come with you?" I requested.

"Sure you can, come on," she told me, standing and taking my hand.

Officer Leigh took me over to her work space and placed me in a chair next to her desk. The chair was hard and dirty and smelled as though someone may have peed their pants while sitting there.

She lifted the receiver of the phone up to her ear, then began pressing buttons to dial a phone number. She fiddled with the coiled cord while she waited for someone to answer. After a couple of moments, the officer swiveled in her chair, so her back was facing me. I assumed she thought by doing that, I would be unable to hear her.

"Hello, my name is Officer Leigh with the Destined County Police Department. I have a six year old girl here that was abandoned at the Tomasina Hotel. She said her mother told her they were playing hide and seek, then her mother just left her there.

"The front desk clerk at the hotel said she saw the two of them come in and walk over to the elevator. The mother placed the girl into the elevator and pressed the button for the top floor. As soon as the doors closed, the mother bolted out of the hotel, leaving the child behind.

"The most information I could get from the child is that her name is Mackenzie, she lives in a house and the next door neighbor is Auntie May and her two children are Jade and Diamond. She said the neighbor called her mother Bec. We could possibly check into Becky, or Rebecca.

"She doesn't know a contact phone number for the neighbor, nor her mother. I am going to need someone to come get her so she has somewhere safe to go," she informed the person on the other end of the line.

"I guess she could stay with me for the night and I could bring her back here with me in the morning. Let me ask her and make sure she is comfortable with that," she said, pulling the phone away from her ear and turning back to face me. "Would it be okay if you stayed with me for the night?"

I shrugged, "I guess so."

She nodded, finished with the phone call, then turned back to me, "looks like you will be coming home with me for the night," she told me, after hanging up the phone.

"What about my mommy?" I asked.

"I don't know sweetie. We will try to find her, but until we do, you will have to go live with another family for a little while," she told me.

"But I get to stay with you for now?" I asked.

"Well, just for tonight. Tomorrow a lady is going to come get you and take you to a nice family to stay with."

"I just want to go home," I cried.

"I'm sorry sweetie, but until we find your mommy, we have to find you a safe place to live. Look, let's go to my house and I'll get you settled in."

"I don't have any clothes, or a toothbrush," I told her.

"We can buy you those things. Would you like to go shopping?" she asked.

"Does my mommy have to pay you back?" I asked.

"No sweetie, it's my treat, okay?"

"Okay, because my mommy can't afford new clothes for me. Auntie May usually gives me the old clothes that don't fit Jade and Diamond anymore," I told her.

"Have you ever had new clothes?" she asked.

"I don't know. I only remember Auntie May bringing clothes over for me that she would tell my mom her kids grew out of."

"Well, I'm going to take you to get new clothes. How does that sound?"

"Are you going to stay with me the whole time?" I asked, worried that I would be left behind again.

"I will be with you the whole time. I won't leave your side," she told me, taking my hand and leading me out to a different vehicle than her police car.

"Who's car is this?" I asked her.

"This is my personal car. When I'm not working, I have my own car to drive around in."

"Do you also have other clothes that don't make you look like a police officer?"

"I sure do. It's only because if I had to sleep with all of this stuff on, I don't think I would be very comfortable," she said, as we both laughed.

She placed me in the back seat, then climbed in behind the wheel. As she drove passed the front doors of the station, where the other officers were still standing around, Officer Bailey waved at me as I scowled at him.

TWO

"So, what kind of stores has your mommy taken you to?" she asked me, as she drove down the street.

"My mommy has never taken me out before. I was surprised when she decided to take me with her this morning. Normally, I go to Auntie May's house," I told her.

"Even on the weekend?"

"What's the weekend? You mean like the end of the week?"

"Weeks are broken up into week days, which is Monday through Friday and weekends, which is Saturday and Sunday."

"I go to Auntie May's house everyday. My week isn't broken up," I told her, looking at my hands.

"Don't you go to school?" Leigh asked.

"Nope. My mommy brings home workbooks that Auntie May does with me. I don't go anywhere."

"What do you learn about?"

"Auntie May taught me to read and write the alphabet. Math is hard, but I know the easy stuff."

"Do you know where your daddy is?"

"I don't even know who he is, but I do know that if anyone talks about him, my mommy gets really mad," I said, as Officer Leigh turned the car into a parking space.

After she stepped out of the car, Leigh opened the back door behind the driver's side of the car and assisted me out. I held her hand all the way to the doors of the store and we walked through the makeup and perfume area toward the back of the store.

"What's your favorite color?" she asked, when we entered the clothing area.

"Green,"I told her.

"Green, great."

She began grabbing shirts and holding them up to my shoulders. "Why do you do that?"

"I'm making sure they will fit. I don't want to buy you something that won't fit," she said, draping several over her arm, then stepping over to the pants.

She grabbed a couple of pairs of pants and held them up to my waist before draping them over her arm with the shirts. After a few moments, we headed over to a hallway with several small rooms.

"Go in and try these pants on to make sure they fit," she told me.

"Will you come in with me?" I asked.

"Of course I will. Pick a room."

I walked down the hall passed several closed doors and peeked into the rooms with open doors, before choosing a large room that would be comfortable for the both of us.

The room had two large mirrors and a plastic bench seat in one corner. Leigh closed the door and sat down on the bench in the room.

"Try these first," she said, handing me one of the pairs of the pants and placing the other clothing on the bench next to her.

Officer Leigh turned toward the door where she could not see me as I tried them on. I removed the pants I had on and changed into the new pair.

"Okay, I'm done," I told her, once I was redressed, so she knew it was safe to turn around.

"Good, let's make sure these fit properly," she said, standing up and stepping in front of the mirror.

The first thing she did was mess around with the waist band for a little while. She was pulling and shifting the pants around my waist.

"Okay sweetie, those seem good. You even have a little room to grow into them. Are they comfortable?" she asked.

"I guess," I told her, not knowing how to respond. "I have never been asked if my clothes were comfortable before."

"Well, how about you change back into the pants you had on before and we can get you some shoes."

"What's wrong with my shoes? I just got these before my birthday," I said, looking down at my well warn sneakers.

"There is a hole in the side of them between the canvas and the rubber sole. I'm sure you would benefit from a pair of shoes that protected your socks from getting wet when it rains," she told me.

"I don't have socks. My mommy says that socks are for people who actually wear shoes for longer than a couple of minutes each day."

"How about we get you some socks as well? It will protect your feet inside your shoes and I'm sure you will be in your shoes for longer than a couple of minutes each day from now on."

"I guess so," I told her, looking down at my feet as tears formed in my eyes.

"What's wrong sweetie?" Leigh asked, watching me in the mirror that was hung on the wall.

"I just hope that when you find my mommy, she isn't mad at me because you bought me new stuff," I said, wiping my face with the bottom of my shirt.

"Don't worry. I will take all the blame and make sure that all her anger is taken out on me. Now, change back so we can get you those new shoes."

Leigh turned on the bench so she was facing the door again and not watching me change as I removed the new pants. I left them in a wad on the floor as I picked up the pants I was wearing before and pulled them back on. I tapped Leigh on the shoulder once I was ready. She picked up the pile of clothing from the seat and the pants off the floor, leading me through the changing area and out of the hallway.

"How about some pajamas? You are going to need something to sleep in. Now that I am sure of your size, we can just pick them up and head to the checkout before going to the shoe store," Leigh said.

I just shrugged as I followed behind her to an area with night clothes. She reached up to a rack and pulled down a pant set with a shirt that had ruffles on the sleeves and it was covered in green unicorns.

"What do you think of this?" she asked.

"I've never been asked what I think about clothes before. I like it because it's green," I said.

"Oh good. Well, I'm going to get you several different ones."

She draped the green unicorns over her arm with the rest of the clothes and took down a couple of other colored unicorn pajama sets from the same rack. One was purple and the other was pink.

Before we headed to the checkout, I pointed to the blue pajama set and Officer Leigh reached up and brought that one down as well. I grabbed her free hand and walked with Officer Leigh up to the front of the store where the cashiers were. She placed the several clothing items down on the counter and we waited for the cashier to scan each price tag. After paying for the clothes, we headed back out to the car and the officer drove me to the shoe store.

"Okay, do you have a favorite type of shoe, or would you like to try on a few pairs to see what feels best?" Leigh asked.

"I don't know. I usually get someone's left over shoes that don't fit," I told her.

Officer Leigh reached down and placed her thumb onto the toe of my shoe. She pressed down on my big toe, which was smashed up against the edge of the shoe.

"These shoes are too small for your feet."

"They make my toes hurt."

"Doesn't Auntie May give you the shoes that don't fit her kids anymore?"

"Nope, she only gives me clothes. The shoes come from someone else. They give them to my mommy and my mommy brings them home. Auntie May says Diamond and Jade wear out their shoes faster than they grow out of them."

"Well, okay then. Let's find out your correct size, then we can find something you might like."

Leigh retrieved a metal foot scale from under a plastic bench at the end of one of the shoe aisles. I sat down on the bench and lifted up my foot. Leigh took off my shoe and placed my bare foot onto the scale. My heel rested back against a curved metal piece on the edge as she slid the side measure against the part of my foot that curved up and slid the top measure against my toe. I didn't know what she was looking at, but she seemed confident in knowing my correct shoe size.

"Okay, check out the displays and find a few styles you like and you can try on shoes that actually fit," Leigh said.

I walked around and looked at several different types of shoes. After I made my selections, Leigh grabbed the boxes with my size printed on the outside and I sat down on the same bench where Leigh had measured my foot.

"First, we need to get a pair of single use socks," Leigh said, reaching into a large bin with what looked like the feet cut off of pantyhose.

I took off the shoes I had on, as she pulled out two single use socks from the bin, then placed them on my feet. I tried on the several pairs of shoes I had chosen before I decided on the ones I liked. She placed the shoes I declined back on the shelves and pulled two packs of socks off a hook on the end of the rows of shoes. Leigh paid for the footwear and we headed to her house.

Leigh pulled into the driveway in front of a simple, single story home. After she exited the vehicle, she opened the back door behind the driver's side and assisted me out of the car. She reached back into the car and retrieved the shopping bags.

Once we were inside her home, Officer Leigh dumped the shopping bags out onto the floor in front of her sofa. The front door opened into her living room and the kitchen was directly behind the living room. To the right of the door, was a hallway that led to the bedrooms.

After taking in my surroundings, I took off my shoes at the front door, then joined the officer on the floor around the pile of clothing. She picked up each item and took the tags off.

"I think this shirt is my favorite," Leigh said, holding up a light pink t-shirt with the words 'I'm Special' printed on the front.

I nodded, not really knowing what to say. After she neatly folded all the clothing into a pile on the floor, she went to her front hall closet and retrieved a green bag to put my new clothes in.

"Come with me. I'll show you the room you will be staying in for the night," she told me, extending her hand to me.

She picked up the bag, packed with the new merchandise and slung it over her shoulder, then took me down a hallway that led to a bedroom. The room was plain with white walls, a white bed frame with black sheets on the bed and that was all. There was nothing else to the room.

"This is my guest room. You can stay here for the night and tomorrow we will find you a more permanent home," she told me.

"I have a home. You just have to find my mommy," I told her.

"We will try, I promise, but until we do, we have to find you somewhere to stay. I told you that, remember?" she told me, placing the bag down on the floor at the foot of the bed.

"Why can't I stay with you?"

"The law has these steps we have to follow when it comes to children. There are special places for lost children to go until we find them a home. Unfortunately, my home is not one of those special places because of my job."

"I thought the police would have the most specialist homes because they are supposed to protect people?"

"Well, the government doesn't see it that way. They think that my job is dangerous and it's not safe for a child," she said, then mumbled under her breath, "unless somehow, miraculously, I were to conceive on my own, but of course that would mean I would need a man in my life. I don't need a man, I can take care of myself."

I just stared at her. She looked down at me before kneeling down to be eye to eye with me.

"I'm sorry sweetie. You don't need to hear my problems. Let's go out to the kitchen and I'll make you something to eat," she said.

We went to her kitchen and she pulled up a chair to the counter for me to stand on so I could help her. She cut up vegetables and I put them into a pot on the stove.

Then she cut up some chicken into bite sized pieces and she pushed the pieces off the cutting board into the pot with the knife. When she was done, she moved me off the chair, added some chicken stock and turned on the stove.

"Stay back while it's cooking because it's hot, okay?" she told me.

She stirred the ingredients for a moment, then led me into the living room. We sat down on her sofa and she turned on the television.

"Do you have a favorite show you like to watch?" Officer Leigh asked.

"My mommy says T.V. makes kids stupid and Auntie May didn't have a T.V. I always played games, or read books at her house," I told her.

"What did you do at home?" Leigh asked, furrowing her brow.

"Sleep," I said, shrugging, staring down at my bare feet.

"Is that all your mommy let you do?"

"Well, she would wake me up in the morning and take me to Auntie May's house. By the time she picked me up to go home, it was bed time."

"So you didn't spend very much time at home?"

"Nope, most of my time was spent with Auntie May. Will I ever see her again?" I asked her, with tears in my eyes.

"Your mommy or Auntie May?" she asked.

"Auntie May, of course. My mommy doesn't love me."

"Why do you think that?"

"She never said it to me, ever. Auntie May made sure to tell me everyday that she loved me before I left her house. My mommy left me at that building because she didn't want me anymore, but Auntie May made sure I was okay before my mommy took me away."

"Do you know why your mommy left you there alone?"

"I don't know for sure, but I guess maybe she didn't want me anymore, or she could be sick and she doesn't want me to get sick."

"Why wouldn't she just leave you with Auntie May?"

"I don't know."

"Let me go check on dinner. I'll be right back," Officer Leigh said, heading into the kitchen.

Three

After dinner, I helped her with the dishes. She filled the sink with soapy water and I placed our dinner dishes into the water. She pulled up a chair and placed it with the back up against the counter. I climbed up, stood on the chair and Leigh handed me a kitchen towel.

"If I wash and rinse, can you dry?" Leigh asked me.

"Sure," I told her.

"Have you ever helped with house work?"

"Auntie May gave me chores along with Diamond and Jade, so I felt like I was part of the family."

"Really? What did you do?"

"I took the trash out of the bathrooms and brought it out to the kitchen trash so Diamond could take the house trash outside," I told her, as she handed me a plate.

"That's neat. Anything else?" Leigh inquired.

"On Saturdays we cleaned the whole house. I got to wipe off all the bottom cabinets and the thingys at the bottom of the walls by the floor. Auntie May would put on music and we would have a fun day even though we were cleaning."

"What about at home with your mommy?"

"I never spent a lot of time at home with my mommy. I don't think my mommy spent a lot of time at home. It was kinda messy."

"Okay well, that needs to soak, so let's go back here and get you cleaned up before bed," she said, taking the towel from me and placing it on the counter.

I jumped down off the chair and waited as Leigh replaced the chair at the small square table she had in the corner of her kitchen. We walked down the hall to the bathroom.

"Do you prefer a bath or a shower?" Leigh asked.

"I think shower. I can do it by myself without help and I can do it quick," I told her.

Officer Leigh turned the knob for the water to run from the faucet. "When you are ready to get in, pull this up and the water will come out from up there."

"I think I can handle that. How would I turn it off?" I asked.

"When you are done, push down on the plunger you pulled up and the water will switch back to the faucet. Turn this knob to the right and the water will turn off."

"Thank you, ma'am. I appreciate you allowing me to stay here."

"Of course sweetie. Now, here is a toothbrush and a tube of toothpaste. I will leave it here on the counter for you. Once you get in, I will bring you a pajama pant set and a towel and leave them folded on top of the toilet for you."

"Okay, thank you."

"I'll be in the living room when you finish. We can watch a movie before you go to bed. Would you like that?" Officer Leigh enquired.

"I guess so," I told her, shrugging my shoulders.

I took my shower, dried off, dressed and brushed my teeth before heading out to the living room. Officer Leigh was finishing up cleaning the kitchen when I came out.

"Okay, how about something animated?"

"What's that? Aminated," I asked.

"Animated, it's a cartoon," she told me.

"So it's a kid movie?"

"Sort of, but I'm a grown up and I like it."

"What's it about?"

"Let me put the tape in and I will let you see the box."

Officer Leigh walked over to the T.V. and put in the movie. Once it was playing, she brought the cover of the movie to me and sat down on the sofa next to me. The title of the movie was, 'The Little Mermaid'.

I turned the box in my hands, looking at the front, back and sides of it, before placing it down on the coffee table and relaxing back into the couch.

After a few moments, I moved down the sofa and leaned my head on her upper arm. When she wrapped her arm around me, I felt safe and cared for. I didn't want to leave, but I knew that the next day, I would probably never see her again. I wanted to soak up all her safety and caring while I was there because I didn't know what the future held for me.

"So, what did you think?" Leigh asked me, when the movie ended.

"It was fun. I liked the songs," I told her. "My favorite part was the dingle hop hop."

"I like the dinglehopper too. Especially when she combs it through her hair," Leigh said, combing her fingers through her hair.

We both giggled and danced around the room singing the song about being where the people are. I could actually relate to the movie. She wanted to be like normal people and to be accepted. I just wanted to have a family and be with people who wanted me.

She took me to the room I was going to be sleeping in and tucked me into bed. She made sure I was comfortable and kissed me on the forehead.

"I would read you a story, but I don't have any children's books," she told me.

"That's okay. I'm used to going to sleep without a story," I said.

Four

The next morning when I woke up, I could smell food cooking. I opened my eyes and looked around the room. At first, in my partially asleep state, I was confused and didn't know where I was. I rubbed my eyes trying to erase the tears that were welling up. Then remembered where I was. I remembered how much fun I had with Officer Leigh the night before and ran out to the kitchen, following the smell of eggs.

"Good morning Mackenzie. Would you like some breakfast?" Officer Leigh asked.

"Yes please," I said, as I climbed up on one of the bar stools set up at her counter.

"Well, all right," she said, placing three sausage links on a plate with two scoops of scrambled eggs and a piece of toast cut from corner to corner into triangles.

"It smells good," I said, sniffing the air.

"Would you like some milk?" she asked, placing the plate in front of me.

I nodded as I began shoveling the food into my mouth. The eggs were completely gone before she even finished pouring the glass of milk.

"Slow down Mackenzie. Your going to get a stomach ache," she said, placing the cup of milk on the counter in front of my plate.

"I can't believe you made this for me. It's so delicious," I said, small bits of food escaping my mouth and landing on the counter in front of me.

"Why not? You have to eat, right? Didn't your mommy ever make you breakfast?"

"Sure, a few times. Sometimes it was a bowl of dry cereal that I had to eat with a cup of water because my mommy says milk is too expensive. Once she bought toaster pastries, but we don't have a toaster, so she said they were garbage."

"You know you can eat toaster pastries right out of the box without a toaster, right?"

"I wasn't allowed to. Once I tried to sneak a package to my room, but the foil packaging made too much noise and I was caught. Boy was my mommy mad."

I had emptied my plate and gulped down my milk before hopping down off the bar stool. Leigh picked up my plate and cup.

"Did you want anymore?" she asked, as I headed down the hallway to the bathroom.

"No thank you," I told her, yelling over my shoulder as I walked away.

I washed my hands and face, brushed my teeth, then went into the bedroom to change my clothes. I dug through the bag of new clothes and picked out the shirt that Officer Leigh said was her favorite and a new pair of pants.

Once I was dressed, I ran back out to the living room, bare foot, where Officer Leigh was waiting for me with a hair brush. She sat on the sofa and I stood in front of her while she brushed my hair.

"You're just like Auntie May," I told her.

"Oh yeah? How's that?" she inquired.

"You take care of me."

"Didn't your mommy take care of you?"

"Not really. She just told me what to do and I had to listen, or she would get mad and yell at me."

"Did she ever hit you?"

"I don't think so. She used to tell me to get away from her before she beat me, but she never did. I always ran to my room, or to Auntie May's house."

"Okay sweetie, I'm all done. Go gather your things, it's almost time to go."

"I don't want to go. I want to stay here with you."

"I told you yesterday, you can't stay with me. It was only for one night. I promise you will go to a nice home with other children to play with. That will be more fun than staying with a grown up."

"But I like it here. I'll be good, I promise," I cried, plopping down on the floor and latching onto her leg.

"How about I check in on you every so often to make sure you're okay?"

"You promise?"

"I promise."

Officer Leigh picked me up and carried me to the room I had slept in. The clothes that she had neatly folded and placed into the bag the night before, were now scattered around the room, from when I was looking for something to wear.

"We are going to have to pick this up first," she said, placing me down on the floor.

She helped me pack my stuff back into the bag she had given me and I helped her make the bed, before we headed out to the car to leave.

She opened the back door behind the driver's side and assisted me into her car. As she placed the bag of all my new things in the trunk, I pulled the seatbelt down over my shoulder and pressed the tongue into the buckle. Officer Leigh made sure I was secure before closing my door and climbing in behind the steering wheel.

"So Mackenzie, do you like sports?" she asked, as she drove me to the police station.

"I like baseball. Auntie May's family comes over and watches the games during baseball season and during the world series. My mommy says sports are for boys, but I like watching it on T.V. with Auntie May and her family," I told her, staring out the window.

"I think baseball is fun. Sports are for everyone, that's why they are on T.V. It's for anyone to watch and it doesn't matter if you are a boy, or a girl, everyone can watch," Leigh said, with a slight anger in her tone.

"Do you know where I'm going to be staying at?" I asked, in order to change the subject.

"No sweetie, I don't. But if you want I can find out before the social worker arrives to take you and I can do a background search on the grown-ups in the house."

I nodded in agreement just as we arrived at the station and Officer Leigh parked her car. She headed around to the trunk first to retrieve my bag. She opened the back door to the car, allowed me to climb out and she scooped me up into her arms, carrying me and my bag inside.

The officer that tried to pull me out of the car the day before, was standing just inside the door. He waved at me and I buried my face into Officer Leigh's neck.

After she checked in with the officer in the front, she took me over to her desk and sat me down in the chair I had occupied the day before, placing my bag down on the floor in front of me. She dialed the phone and waited.

"Hello, this is Officer Leigh from the Destined County Police Department. I called yesterday about a little girl left at a hotel by her mother," she said, to the person on the other end of the line. "Okay, do you know who the family is that she will be staying with? I would like to look into them in order to reassure her. Right. I got it. Yes, I'll be here. Thank you," she said, before hanging up the phone.

"Okay Mackenzie, a social worker will be here shortly to take you to a temporary home. You will stay there until they can find you long term foster care."

"Who am I going to be staying with?" I asked.

"She said the woman you are staying with is Betty Warren. I'm looking her up now to see if she has ever been in trouble. The lady I talked to said she is still gathering your file together, so you could be hanging out with me here for a little while today," she told me.

"I would rather stay with you."

"Mackenzie, I can ask, but I told you, the foster care system seems to think that my job is too demanding and dangerous for me to bring a child into my home. From what I can see, I promise that the family you are going to be staying with has had a lot of children in their home. Could you at least give it a try?"

"Okay, but what if I don't like Betty Warren, or the other children in the house?"

"How about I go with you and we meet them to-gether?" she asked.

"You would do that?" I inquired.

"Absolutely, I want to make sure you're comfortable before I give you to someone. You let me know what you think and I will feel better about you staying there."

I nodded as a woman with short brown hair wearing a grey pant suit approached us and stepped up next to Officer Leigh's desk.

"Hello, I'm Janet Russell. I'm from social services, here for Mackenzie," the lady told Officer Leigh, extending her hand.

"This here is Mackenzie," Officer Leigh said, motioning toward me and shaking Janet Russell's hand.

"Well, hello there Mackenzie, I'm Janet Russell. Can you tell me what your last name is?" she asked me.

I stood up and straightened my clothes before extending my hand to the social worker. "I'm just Mackenzie. I don't have other names," I told her, sternly, before sitting back down in the chair and staring at my lap.

"Okay," Janet said, standing back up to talk to Officer Leigh. "Well, I need more information in order to put her in the system."

"Well, her mother abandoned her and didn't exactly leave a note with all her information on it," the officer told Janet.

"Can I use your name?" I practically whispered.

"What's that sweetie?" Officer Leigh asked me.

"Can I use your name? I could be Makenzie Leigh," I requested.

"I don't mind. Janet, is that okay?" she asked the social worker.

"Temporarily, it's okay. We can fix it on her paperwork once we find her mother."

"Well, there you go. You are now known as Mackenzie Leigh," Officer Leigh said, smiling at me.

I looked at the social worker. "Can I stay with her now?" I requested.

"I'm sorry, but no. Officer Leigh has a very demanding job and it is not safe for you to stay with her. I can assure you though, we have found a very nice family for you to stay with. There are other children there as well, so you will have some friends to play with," Janet informed me.

"I would like to go with you when you take her to meet Mrs. Warren and the children in her home, so I can tell them the little bit that I know about her personality and help her get settled in," Officer Leigh requested.

"That would be okay. First, I will need a photo of you. Is that okay Mackenzie?" Janet asked.

"Yes ma'am," I told her.

Janet held a camera up to her face so she could look through the viewer and aimed it at me. She pressed the button on top of the camera and captured my look of sadness. I blinked in order to eradicate the flash blindness temporarily burned into my retinas, as the photo emerged from a slot in the front of the camera.

Officer Leigh picked up my bag off the floor and slung it over her shoulder. She grabbed my hand as I hopped up off the chair and escorted me out to the social worker's car. Leigh strapped me into the back seat behind the passenger side that time. She put my bag into the trunk, then took her place in the seat in front of me. Janet climbed in behind the steering wheel and started the car.

"Mackenzie, do you know when your birthday is?" Janet asked, as she drove.

"April twenty," I told her.

"You know your birthday, but you don't know your last name?" Janet scoffed.

"Everybody always called me Mackenzie, or Kenzie. Auntie May would make me a cupcake and put a number candle on it for my age and told me I was born April twenty and that was a special day to her," I said, through clenched teeth.

"Why was that day so special to *her*?" Janet asked.

"Because that was the day *I* came into her life."

"Who is Auntie May to you?" Janet inquired.

"She's the lady who lives next door and takes care of me everyday," I explained.

"If Auntie May takes care of you everyday, what happened yesterday?"

"I don't know. My mommy took me away yesterday. I only got to wave at Auntie May as my mommy drove away with me in the back seat. I don't know why. She had never taken me anywhere before. I always go to Auntie May's house."

"I wonder what changed yesterday that made her decide to get rid of her little girl," Janet said to Officer Leigh.

"That would be a discussion best left for when she is no longer in the car," Officer Leigh told Janet.

"My mommy got a note in the mail that made her very angry with me. When she picked me up from Auntie May's house a other day, she grabbed me by the arm and dragged me home. I almost falled down in the yard. Then she yelled at me to go to bed when we got inside the house."

"How did you know about the note?" Janet asked me.

"When my mommy thought I was in bed, she called someone on the phone and I heard her say that bastard sent her a letter saying he was getting out," I told her.

"Well, aren't you an observant little girl," Janet said, peering at me through the rear view mirror.

"Officer Leigh," I began.

"Yes sweetie," she replied.

"What's bastard?" I asked.

"That's a grown up word."

"So I shouldn't say it, right?"

"Right," she said, chuckling.

The rest of the ride I was looking out the window, crying quietly, while Officer Leigh and the social worker whispered to each other from the front seat. I was nervous going to a stranger's house seeing as I never really met new people.

I wiped my face with the bottom of my shirt as I imagined my mother throwing a party at home since I wasn't there anymore. Auntie May was probably very worried about me since my mommy came back without me.

Janet stopped the car in front of a white painted home. I looked out the side window of the car and watched as a wide lady with short brown hair, emerged

from the house. Several children, all different ages, followed behind her.

"Hello Janet. I'm so excited to be able to house another child for you. How's Derik doing?" the lady
asked, as Janet exited the vehicle.

Officer Leigh got out of the car and opened the door
for me. She knelt down next to the car and placed her
hand on my knee.

"Come on Mackenzie. Let's go meet the lady who is
going to be taking care of you for a little while," Officer
Leigh said, as I looked passed her to the house.

I pressed the button to release my seat belt and
turned to let my legs hang out of the car, before slowly
sliding off the seat and placing my feet on the ground.
Officer Leigh grabbed my bag from the trunk and held
my hand as we approached the lady that came out of the
house.

"Is there a problem?" the lady asked Officer Leigh,
due to the uniformed officer escorting me.

"No ma'am, there's no problem. I'm the officer who
responded to the call of an abandoned child and she
stayed with me last night. I thought I could help her get
acclimated to her new surroundings and share with you
the little information I have been able to gather with the
little time I have been with her," Leigh informed.

"Okay, let's go inside. She can go with the other
children and we can talk," the lady said.

The large woman took a few moments to turn
around and the other children went into the house in
front of her. Janet Russell followed the woman and
Leigh grabbed my hand, leading me up the front walk

toward the house and up the three steps to the front porch. We walked inside and to the living room.

The house was small and a little cramped inside with the furniture. There was a wrap around sofa where all of the other children were sitting on together and looking down at their hands on their laps. On the short end of the sofa was a wide chair that was big enough for two people, but I was sure it was for Betty Warren to sit on. I stood in front of the chair as Janet and Leigh walked over and stood next to the long end of the sofa. The television was encased in a wooden cabinet that sat on the floor facing the short end of the sofa.

"First things first," the lady said, sitting down in her large chair in front of me and leaning forward toward me. "My name is Betty Warren. You will be staying with me for a little while. Is that okay?"

I walked over and grabbed onto Officer Leigh's leg, turning my face away from Betty Warren. Officer Leigh placed her hands on my shoulders and pulled me away from her leg. She knelt down in front of me as Betty Warren leaned back in her chair.

"Now Mackenzie, I need you to be as respectful to Mrs. Warren as you have been to me, okay," Officer Leigh requested.

I nodded, then walked over to Betty Warren. "Hello ma'am. My name is Mackenzie Leigh. I appreciate you opening your home to me so I can have a safe place to sleep and a hot meal to eat. Thank you," I told her.

"Well, that was very nice. How about you go play in the next room with the other children while I talk with Janet and this nice police officer," Betty told me, as she played with my hair.

I nodded as the other children stood up and headed toward the back of the house. Following behind them, we walked past the dining room and entered a room filled with toys. The toys in the room were, in my opinion, for children up to the age of four and the six other children in the house were very visibly older than I was.

Four boys and two girls. The girls went over to a play house and a play kitchen and the boys went over to play with a race track setup. The children played without speaking to each other, while I sat down on the floor near the door and just watched the other kids play for a little while. I pressed my back up against the wall and hugged my knees.

After a few moments, the oldest girl walked across the room and stood in front of me. "Hi, I'm Angela."

"I'm Mackenzie," I replied.

"Would you like to play with us?" Angela asked.

"Sure," I said, standing up and walking across the room to play with the girls.

"Hi, I'm Gwen," said the other girl.

While the grown-ups talked in the living room, I tried to get better acquainted with the other children. I wanted to know about the woman I would be living with for a while.

"Is Mrs. Warren nice?" I asked, as I picked up fake plastic food and placed it in a plastic frying pan on the fake stove, pretending to play.

"As long as you follow her rules, it's fine, but if you question her, she doesn't like that," Gwen told me.

"What does that mean?" I wondered.

"Mrs. Warren doesn't like us talking inside the house. We will need to talk about this during yard time," Angela warned.

"Why not?" I asked.

"I will tell you later, when we are outside, where we are allowed to talk," Angela said.

"Do you know how long I will be here?" I wanted to know.

"If you were a boy, I would say not long, but because you are a girl, you could be here for years before you are able to escape," Angela said. "I have been here longer than I've wanted to be. Some of the boys come and go so fast, I don't even have time to remember their names."

"Escape? What do you mean by that?" I inquired.

"It's a long story. Wait until yard time. For now, be quiet before she comes in here," Angela told me.

We continued to pretend to play, while Janet Russell, Officer Leigh and Betty Warren discussed my stay.

Five

After a while, Officer Leigh came into the room and I ran over to her. She knelt down and I hugged her.

"Mrs. Warren seems like a nice lady. I made her promise that she would let you call me any time you want to. If you ever need to talk, please just let her know and she will help you with the phone, okay?" Officer Leigh told me, handing me a small card. "This has my phone number on it. I want you to hold onto this and anytime you need me, please call me."

I nodded and noticed the tears filling her eyes. I placed my hand on her cheek and kissed her forehead. It was the same thing Auntie May did to me when I was sad.

Officer Leigh took my hand and led me out to the living room where Betty Warren and Janet Russell were standing. Janet handed Betty my bag, then knelt down to get eye to eye with me.

"Mrs. Warren is going to show you to your room and get you settled in. Officer Leigh says she will come visit often to make sure you are comfortable. Here is my card. There is a number on there you dial on the telephone if you have an emergency, okay? Do you know how to use a telephone?" Janet asked me.

"I know how to dial nine one one," I told her.

"Good, that's good," Betty said. "Okay, well how about you tell them good bye and I will show you to your room."

I nodded to Mrs. Warren and hugged Officer Leigh one more time, then I turned to Janet, stood in front of her and asked, "how long am I going to be staying here?"

"That depends on how long it takes to find you long term housing, why?" Janet wondered.

"Well, Angela says she has been here a long time, but the boys seem to come and go quickly. Sometimes they leave so fast, she doesn't have time to remember their names."

"Well, Angela has special needs and it's harder to find placement for children with special needs," Betty Warren told me.

"If Angela has special needs, we are going to need to find her special needs housing," Janet said, taking notes.

"Her social worker says I am taking good care of her and she is fine with her staying here. She has been here for a couple of years and has settled in nicely. Her social worker has decided there is no reason to uproot her from the home she has come to get use to," Betty told her.

"I will check with her social worker and make sure she is checking on her regularly," Janet mentioned.

"Don't worry, she is going to be here in a couple of days. I will ask her about Angela and have her contact you," Betty said, herding Janet Russell and Officer Leigh out the front door.

I walked toward the door with Janet, Betty and Officer Leigh. I tried to wave at them as they left, but Mrs. Warren made sure to get her very large body between them and me. I stepped over to the front window, squeezing in behind the sofa and watched as the social worker and police officer left me in a stranger's home. Betty Warren closed the door and it didn't matter how many people lived in the house, I felt alone.

"Let's go. Pick up your bag, follow me and I will show you where you'll be sleeping," Betty said.

I grabbed the handle of the duffle bag that Officer Leigh had given me and dragged it across the floor following her down the hallway, as she waved her hand towards herself beckoning me.

I walked behind Betty Warren down a hallway where there were four bedrooms. The bedrooms were to the right down the hallway, with one open door at the end, directly in front of us. Each room was missing the door.

The first room we walked passed had the walls painted blue along with two sets of bunk beds in order for four children to sleep in there. The sheets on each bed were identical, navy blue and sports themed. The room was clean and the beds were made. It didn't look like anyone stayed in the room.

The next room we walked passed had the walls painted green and like the other room had two sets of bunk beds for four children. The sheets on these beds were dinosaur themed. Same as the room before, it was spotless and the beds were made as though no one was staying in that room.

The third room we walked passed had the walls painted pink and the entire room was princess themed. There were only two beds in that room and like the others, it appeared as though no one was staying in that room.

The last room on the right at the end of the hallway was the one that Mrs. Warren took me into. The walls were painted purple and the entire room was mermaid themed. There were again only two beds, but it didn't appear as though anyone else was staying in that room.

She grabbed my arm and flung me into the room when I peeked into the open doorway at the end of the hall. I noticed it was a bathroom before she pulled me away. I placed my bag on the floor in front of the dresser, before looking around the room and taking in my surroundings. Just like the four bedrooms, the door was also missing from the bathroom.

"You will be sleeping in this room. Every morning you are expected to make your bed exactly as you see it now. If it is not done correctly, you will be expected to do it again until it is correct. No toys or writing utensils of any kind are allowed in the room. If you are caught with contraband of any kind you will face consequences. Do you understand," Betty said, in a stern tone of voice.

"No, I don't," I told her.

"No, you don't what? Understand?" she asked.

"No, I don't understand. I don't know what contraband is," I informed her with a sassy attitude.

The contact of her hand against the left side of my face almost knocked me off my feet. I stumbled into the wall, catching myself and standing upright. I placed my hand against my cheek as it stung.

"Your attitude is not going to fly here. You better watch how you talk to me. Do you understand that, or are you just stupid?" Betty told me, wagging her finger in my face, so close she almost hit my nose.

I nodded that time, then walked over to sit on the bed. She grabbed my arm and stopped me from touching the bed in any way.

"Don't you dare mess up that bed. Put away your stuff, then come out and join the rest of us. You are not allowed to be in your room unless it is bed time," she said, staring into my eyes with her furrowed brows.

Mrs. Warren turned, then waddled out of the room, leaving me alone. I unzipped the bag and began putting my clothes in the supplied dresser. I opened one of the small top drawers and placed my clothes in carefully so I didn't mess up the folding job Officer Leigh had done. Since the only clothes I had were enough for about ten days, I felt as though the small drawer was sufficient enough.

Once I had finished, I placed my bag on the floor and slid it under the bed. I pulled Officer Leigh and Janet Russell's cards out of the pocket of my pants and very carefully, without disturbing the sheets, slid them under the pillow. I wanted to make sure I wasn't caught with them and they were taken from me. I walked over to the window and split the slats in the blinds in order to look out for a moment. I was looking out at the side of the house and noticed the neighbor was close by. It was almost as if I were to reach out the window, I could probably touch their siding.

I didn't want Mrs. Warren to think I was hanging out in the room and get into trouble, so I moved away from the window and walked out of the room in order to join the others in the living room. The other children were just sitting on the couch, staring at the floor as if they were waiting for something.

I walked over and sat on the floor in front of the sofa between Angela and Gwen's feet. Within moments, Mrs. Warren came into the room.

"Get up," she ordered.

We all stood up. I looked at her, awaiting instructions, while the other children stared at the floor.

"Since you all were playing with the toys, every one of you needs to go into the toy room and clean up."

We started to walk toward the toy room, but it wasn't fast enough for Betty. "Now!" she yelled.

We ran toward the room and immediately began picking up the toys. Once we were done, Angela and Gwen grabbed my hands and led me into the kitchen. Angela grabbed three cleaning cloths while Gwen reached under the sink and retrieved three bottles of spray cleaner.

Angela gave one cloth to me and one to Gwen. Gwen passed each of us a bottle of cleaner. They led me back into the toy room, where we began spraying and wiping down each toy. Two boys were sweeping the floor and one was dusting the blinds and the furniture. The fourth boy was no where to be seen, but I was sure he was somewhere in the house.

"What's going on?" I asked.

"Be quiet or she'll put you in the naughty closet," Angela told me.

"What's the naughty closet?" I wanted to know.

"Why is there talking going on in here?" Betty came in angrily.

"I'm sorry Mrs. Warren. I told her we had to be quiet," Angela told her.

"Mackenzie, there are rules in this house that must be followed. If you break those rules, there are consequences," Mrs. Warren explained. "Angela, you need to teach her the rules, NO TALKING!"

"How is she supposed to teach me the rules if we aren't allowed to talk?" I asked.

"Is that a sassy attitude?" Mrs. Warren said, stepping into my personal space.

I shook my head instead of speaking, in fear that she would slap me again, then went back to cleaning like the rest of them. Mrs. Warren stood in the doorway watching us.

"When you are finished here, you can all go in and clean your rooms," she said, before turning and leaving the room.

When we finished cleaning the toy room, I followed Angela and Gwen down the hallway to our rooms.

The one boy who didn't help clean the toy room was standing in the doorway of the first room. One of the other boys joined him in the first room and the younger two went into the second room. Angela and Gwen went into the third room and I was by myself in the fourth room.

The room I was in looked pretty clean to me, so I didn't know exactly what I was supposed to do. At first, I set down my spray bottle and cloth on the dresser and headed back over to look out the window. I split the slats in the blinds to look out and turned slightly to my right. The street was close to the window, but I knew the other rooms had to be closer. The fence to the back yard was directly to my left. I could barely see cars drive by, but I did see flashes as they passed in my line of sight.

I didn't know if Mrs. Warren was going to come in and check our cleaning, so I walked over to the dresser and picked up my cleaning supplies. I just repeated what I did in the toy room. I sprayed my cloth and wiped every surface in the room.

Once I had finished, I peeked out into the hallway and saw Angela and Gwen standing in their doorway, holding their spray bottles and cloths, staring at the floor. I walked over and stood in front of them.

"What do we do when we are done?" I asked them.

"We wait quietly," Angela said, without looking up from the floor.

I walked back over to my doorway and leaned against the doorframe looking out toward the boys rooms. I set the spray bottle down on the floor and placed the cloth over the sprayer. It wasn't long before the boys were done as well and they mimicked the other two girls. We just stood there waiting for so long, my legs started to get tired. I sat down on the floor and began picking at the fibers in the carpet. Mrs. Warren appeared at the opening of the hallway and immediately began screaming.

"What do you think you are doing?" she yelled, as I stood back up.

"I'm tired," I complained.

"Is that backtalk?" she said, stomping down the hallway toward me.

"No ma'am. I'm just expressing my feelings. Auntie May says it's healthy to get your feelings out and let the others around you know so they can respond accordingly," I explained.

"Well, you aren't at Auntie May's house anymore. This is Momma Warren's house and you will address me as such. Did everyone hear me?" she yelled down the hallway.

"Yes, Momma Warren," all the other children replied in unison, still looking at the floor.

"Good, now if everyone is done cleaning their rooms, go wash for dinner. Except you Mackenzie. Give me your cleaning supplies." I passed her the cloth and spray bottle. "Now, you can go to bed," she said and turned to walk away.

"But, I'm hungry," I wined.

"You said you were tired, so it's time for bed. Put on your pajamas and brush your teeth. I'll be back as soon as the other children have settled for dinner."

"This isn't fair," I said, stomping my foot.

"I warned you," Betty Warren said, before slapping me across the face a second time that day. "Now, do as you're told, or it's going to get worse."

In fear of what she might say, or do if I spoke again, I kept quiet as she walked down the hall and out of sight.

As soon as the other children were finished in the bathroom and had made their way out of the hallway to go eat, I washed and dressed for bed. As I laid down and waited for Mrs. Warren to come back, I pulled the card that Officer Leigh had given to me out from under the pillow. Even though I only spent one night at her house, at that moment I missed Officer Leigh and began to cry. When I heard Mrs. Warren stomp her way down the hallway, I slid the card under my pillow just as she came in the room and she was angry.

"Why are you crying?" she yelled at me.

"I want my mommy," I said, between sobs.

"Yeah, well your mommy doesn't want you, so you better get over it and fast. There is no crying in my house," she said, leaving the room.

I didn't understand why she was so angry at me, nor did I understand why she had become so mean after Officer Leigh and Janet Russell had left. I was lucky enough that when my mommy had become angry at me, she would take me to Auntie May's house and I didn't have to endure her wrath. I had nowhere else to go to hide from this woman and I had no idea how far Mrs. Warren would eventually go with abusing me if I didn't conform to her idea of how a child should behave.

Six

I began to hold back my tears and tell myself I was going to be just fine. I was only able to sleep for a few minutes at a time that first night. The first time I had dozed off, I was awaken by the sound of the other children running down the hallway toward their bedrooms and Mrs. Warren screaming at them.

"You have exactly ten minutes to get in your beds before I come back there. Whoever is not in their bed, will spend the entire night in the naughty closet," she shouted.

I lifted my head and watched as the girls ran passed my open bedroom door, as they went into the bathroom first, to brush their teeth and use the toilet. I slowly slid out of bed and tip toed to the bathroom.

"Angela," I said, from the doorway.

"Go back to bed Mackenzie, before you get us into trouble," Angela said, after spitting the toothpaste out of her mouth into the running water.

"I just need to ask you a question," I told her.

"Tomorrow, during yard time," Angela said, before replacing her toothbrush back into her mouth.

"That is, if you don't get into trouble before now and after breakfast chores and end up not being able to go outside with us," Gwen said, with her right hand balled into a fist and placed on her hip.

I looked down at the floor and slowly walked back to the bedroom. I sat down on the bed and waited. When the girls had finished and passed by my door again, heading toward their room, I heard someone knock twice on the wall in the hallway. At that point, the boys ran from their bedrooms, past my room and into the bathroom.

"Three minutes," Mrs. Warren shouted from the living room.

The boys quickly completed their bathroom time and ran back to their bedrooms just in time for Mrs. Warren to come down the hall.

"Times up," she said, from the opening of the hallway.

I listened as her heavy footsteps went room to room, stopping for a few seconds at a time making sure all the children were in their beds, before continuing on to the next room. I pulled the blanket over my head as she stopped at the doorway to my room, but didn't come through the room.

She sighed heavily and grunted before turning to head back down the hall. I waited a few moments to be sure she was gone before slipping out of bed and tiptoeing to the doorway, slowly peeking out and down the hall. As I noticed the hallway was empty, I snuck out of the room and into the room of Angela and Gwen. Before stepping up next to Angela's bed, I peeked out the doorway and down the hall one more time to be sure Mrs. Warren hadn't heard me. As soon as I was positive she wasn't coming back, I took the time I had and tapped Angela on the shoulder.

"Angela," I whispered.

She turned over to look at me. "What are you doing in here, Mackenzie? You're going to get us in trouble," she said.

"I'm scared and I don't want to be alone," I told her, holding back my tears.

"It doesn't matter what you want. If Mrs. Warren finds you in here, all three of us are going to get a beating. Go back to bed before she comes back."

"Comes back?" I asked.

"Yes, she checks on us every few hours to make sure we are still in bed. Once, I was in the bathroom during bed checks and she beat me so badly I had to wear pants for almost a month to cover up the marks so my social worker didn't see them. Look, go back to bed and we can talk tomorrow during yard time. I will tell you how to survive here and how to get out. Now go," Angela told me.

I nodded, then tip toed to the bedroom door, peeking out to ensure the hallway was clear. Sneaking back to my room, I slowly slid back under the covers and reached under my pillow to hold Officer Leigh's card in my hand. Most of the night, I laid awake. Each time Mrs. Warren came down the hallway, her footsteps were heavy and loud. Even if I was able to get to sleep, I was awoken by the sound of her coming down the hall. I pulled the covers up around my neck and squeezed my eyes shut every time she came into my room and stepped up to my bed, in fear of what she would do to me if she knew I was awake.

Before the sun came up the next morning, Mrs. Warren came stomping down the hallway blowing a whistle. I could hear the other children scrambling to their doorways, so I got up and headed to my doorway. We all stood with our heads down awaiting instruction.

"Good morning children," Mrs. Warren yelled like a drill sergeant.

"Good morning, Momma Warren," we all said back, with the nom de plume she insisted we called her.

"Make your beds, clean your rooms, wash up, get dressed and come out for breakfast. Don't forget, everyone comes out at the same time. If one of you is slower than the others, assist that one. If I have to come back here to get you, there will be consequences."

We all went back into our rooms and did as we were instructed. I made the bed before changing out of my pajamas and dressing for the day. Neatly, I folded my night clothes and placed them on the end of my bed. I was done first and went into Gwen and Angela's room to see if they needed any help. They were already dressed and in the process of making their beds.

"Hey Angela, Gwen," I said.

"Stop talking. Just wait in the doorway until we are done," Angela told me.

"Why aren't we allowed to talk?" I asked.

"Not in the house. I told you last night, we will talk during yard time," Angela said.

"We can only talk outside," Gwen said.

"That's enough," Angela emphasized, through clenched teeth. "Come on. I need to check to make sure your bed is made properly."

We walked over to my room and Angela tightened the blanket on the bed. When we were done, we stepped out into the hallway. I stood in the doorway of my room as Angela joined Gwen in the doorway of their room, at the same time as all four boys. We lined up and headed out of the hallway.

The seven of us all walked out to the breakfast area at the same time. We circled around a table with four chairs lined up on one side, four chairs lined up on the other side, as well as a chair on each end. The four boys were on one side and us three girls were across the table from them. I started to pull out the chair in front of me, but Angela touched my arm and stopped me. I looked around and noticed everyone else standing behind the chairs, waiting.

Mrs. Warren emerged from the kitchen with a tray full of food. Eggs, bacon, pancakes and potatoes. She stepped up to a chair on one end, next to the oldest boy and placed the tray down on the edge of the table. The older boy stepped behind the end chair and pulled it out for Betty Warren to sit down.

"Girls, have you forgotten your role?" Mrs. Warren asked.

I followed Angela and Gwen into the kitchen. Angela snapped her fingers and motioned for me to open the drawer next to the refrigerator. The drawer contained cloth napkins, to which I pulled out eight. Gwen opened the drawer next to the napkins and she produced eight sets of cutlery. Since Angela was the tallest, she reached up into the upper cabinet and pulled eight plates out, placing them on the counter, in order to get a better grip on them.

"Sit down boys. No reason to stand around while we wait for the girls to get it together," Mrs. Warren said, as we were on our way back out to the table.

The boys pulled their chairs out and the oldest boy pulled the chair out for Mrs. Warren. They were seated at the table just in time for their place settings.

Angela went around the table and passed out the plates, beginning with the youngest boy and making her way around the table where the last plate was placed in the spot where I would be sitting. Gwen followed behind Angela, passing out the silverware. I followed suit with the napkins.

"Thank you girls. Please, join us," Mrs. Warren instructed.

Slowly and without saying a word, we pulled out our chairs and joined the others at the table. Mrs. Warren initiated us to hold hands placing her hands palms up in front of Angela and the older boy.

"Thank you Lord, for this bounty we are about to receive as the nourishment of our bodies and forgive us from our sins. Watch over us as we go through our day and keep us safe. Amen," she lead us in prayer.

The boys began passing their plates down to Mrs. Warren as she dished out breakfast. Once the plates were passed back to the boys, Gwen reached over and stacked my plate on top of hers before passing them to Angela. Angela placed the stack of plates on the edge of the table near Mrs. Warren so she could dish out breakfast for the girls as well.

Once we all had a plate in front of us, we picked up our utensils and began. We ate in silence, that was until I forked a syrup soaked piece of pancake that was too big and it fell off my utensil and landed on the white table cloth.

"What is wrong with you?" Mrs. Warren shouted at me, as she slid the chair back away from the table as fast as her ham hoc legs would allow.

I quickly grabbed the piece off the table with my bare hand and stuffed it into my mouth. She struggled as she stood up from her chair. Her round belly bumped the table and the other kids scrambled to make sure nothing spilled over. As she stomped over behind my chair, the wheezing coming from her mouth made me nervous.

Pulling my chair away from the table, she pushed me, in the chair, into the corner of the dining room. My knees banged the wall. She had pushed me up so close, I couldn't move my legs. I held back tears as I turned and watched her waddle over and clear away my place setting. Using my napkin, she rubbed at the spot I had left on the table cloth.

Once she was satisfied, she tossed the napkin on the plate, then walked into the kitchen and placed my plate into the sink. After she made her way back out to the table, she rejoined the other children and they were able to finish eating.

"Turn around and face the wall!" Betty Warren yelled at me, when she noticed I was looking at them.

I turned back and stared at the corner. As each child finished eating, I could hear the clanging of their cutlery as they stacked it onto their plates. One by one the children consumed the entirety of their breakfast, then each of them cleared their dishes from the table.

Once all the dishes were placed in the sink, I turned around and watched as the other six children lined up in front of the kitchen opening. They stood with their hands behind their backs, looking down at the floor, awaiting instructions.

"Angela, you're in charge of washing the dishes. Gwen, I need you to take the table cloth off the table and spray it with a spot treatment before placing it in the washing machine. Boys, you have the same chores as always. Now get to it," Mrs. Warren told them.

She remained in her seat at the table. After Gwen had pulled the table cloth off the table, one boy came by and sprayed cleaner on the surface, as another boy wiped it down. I watched as a third boy took the vacuum and ran it over the vinyl flooring as the fourth boy waited to mop.

Once all the children were done, Mrs. Warren stood up from her chair and walked over to the corner where I was sitting. She grabbed ahold of the chair and dumped me out of it onto the floor, then replaced it back to the table.

"Everyone get outside, it's yard time," she said, gruffly.

One of the older boys helped me to my feet as another boy opened the sliding glass door and ushered us outside before he closed it. All seven of us ran out into the backyard and as far as we could get from the house. The yard was fenced in and plain. There weren't any toys or fun things for us to play with. I followed the other children as they led me into a far corner of the yard behind an old rusty shed.

There was probably five feet between the back wall of the shed and the fence line. They had it set up like a hiding spot. There was a plastic tarp being used as a front door. It was strung up between the fence lining the yard and the shed, in order to be used for walls. Some old wood that appeared as though it use to be part of the fence, but had been replaced, was being used to block the other opening and had been placed along the top as a makeshift roof. Surprisingly, there was enough room for all of us to sit down in a circle. Gwen was on my left with Angela next to her. The oldest boy was next to Angela and the three others between us.

"Okay, now we can talk," Angela said.

"Why aren't we allowed to talk in the house?" I asked.

"We will get to that. First, you know my name is Angela. I'm eleven years old and I have been here for several years. She won't let me leave because I am terrified of her and no matter what, I do what I'm told. I don't ask questions and I don't talk back. I am her perfect robot and she doesn't want to lose the one who actually obeys her. She tells everyone I have special needs because no one wants to take care of a child with special needs if they don't have to," Angela stated.

"You know me, I'm Gwen. I'm nine years old and have been here for two years. I learn quick and know when to keep my mouth shut. As long as you don't talk back to Mrs. Warren, she's not too bad. She's just loud and large," Gwen informed.

"I'm Brian. I'm ten and have only been here a couple of months. I hate it here and hope my social worker is able to find me permanent housing soon. I think Mrs.

Warren only showers once a week because sometimes, she smells," the boy to my right said.

"I'm Alex. I'm eight and I got here two weeks before Brian. I hate it here too, but I like sharing a room with Brian," the next boy said.

"I'm Jimmy. I'm twelve. This one here is my brother Jack. He's thirteen. We have been here about a year and Mrs. Warren is doing a lot to keep those around who do what they are told without question. We don't talk much, so she wants to keep us here," the boy next to Alex said.

"Before you got here, There was a boy here that refused to do anything without asking why first. He was only here a few days and was confined to his room most of the time. I don't remember his name, but I do know she told the social worker he was a problem child and was refusing to follow the rules. The next day, the social worker showed up and took him away," Angela explained.

"His name was Derik. He was eight and he didn't want to be this bitch's maid," Jack said.

"Jack, she's six. Watch your mouth," Angela chastised.

"Is this your clubhouse?" I asked.

"Clubhouse, that's cute. We call this our safe space," Angela said.

"So, why aren't we allowed to talk in the house?" I wanted to know.

"Mrs. Warren says children should be seen and not heard," Jack contributed.

"So, if I continue to do things she doesn't like, does that mean I will get to leave?" I inquired.

"Not necessarily. The boys, yes, but you're a girl. The girls can be beaten down, whereas the boys are stronger than she is. That could mean she will beat you until you comply. That's what she did to me. I had to cover up my marks any time the social worker came for a home visit. She doesn't beat the boys," Angela said.

"What happens if you tell on her?" I asked.

"She explains it away. With Mia, it was because she was a spoiled child and she didn't want to do the chores she was assigned. The social worker was trying to find another placement for her, but Mia was sixteen and after two weeks she couldn't wait any longer and she ran away. After that, we don't know what happened to her," Angela explained.

"How did she run away?" I wondered.

"She waited until after first bed checks, then snuck out her bedroom window. She was able to fool Mrs. Warren with wadded up blankets under her comforter throughout the night when she did bed checks. The next morning when Mrs. Warren came down the hall to wake us up, she realized Mia was gone and called her social worker," Angela informed.

"I have Officer Leigh I could stay with. If I told Janet that Mrs. Warren hits the kids in her house, you think she would let me stay with Officer Leigh for a few days?" I asked.

"Probably not. Mrs. Warren could tell her that you have an active imagination and that you might not be a good fit for her house. In turn, you could end up here for a couple of weeks after that until your social worker finds you another placement. Mrs. Warren is supposed to be short term housing. Unfortunately, if she decides you are worth keeping around, she will tell the social worker you are a troubled child and you need special attention. She will insist that she is the only one able to control troubled children and most of the social workers agree after she talks to them," Angela said.

"What did you do to end up living with Mrs. Warren?" I asked Angela.

"I didn't do anything," Angela began. "My parents died in a car accident. They were hit by a drunk driver."

"Do you have any other family you could stay with?" Jack asked, touching her hand.

"My grandparents are too old to take care of me and neither one of my parents had any other family. My mother was pregnant with my little sister when she died, so just like my parents, I'm an only child and have no one to take care of me," Angela said, looking down at Jack's hand.

"I am your family," Gwen said, placing her hand on Angela's shoulder, as one lone tear dripped off her cheek.

"When I turn eighteen and finally get out of here, I only have to take care of myself. Of course Gwen will always have a place to stay with me," Angela concluded.

"Did you do something to get placed here?" Gwen asked me.

"My mommy decided she didn't want me anymore, so she took me into a tall building and left me there," I told them.

"Dang, your mother just straight up abandoned you? That is crazy," Jimmy said.

"Yup, and the lady at the hotel, she called Officer Leigh to come get me," I told them.

"I'm pretty sure she probably called the cops and Officer Leigh was just the one who responded to the call," Brian said.

"I don't know, but I got to stay with her at her house that night," I told them.

"That's crazy. Was her house full of guns and cop stuff?" Alex inquired.

"No, it was pretty normal," I said. "How about you two? How did y'all end up living here?" I asked Jack and Jimmy.

"We were left home alone for several weeks until the neighbors figured out that our parents hadn't come back and called the police. We were seven and eight then and the court awarded us to the state when it took a year to find our parents. They were sent to jail for five years for child neglect and have to take parenting classes in order to get us back. Since their release a month ago, we get supervised visits with them twice a month, but we have only seen them once and our social worker said they still haven't signed up for the parenting classes," Jack said.

"So someday y'all could go back and live with your parents?" I asked Jack, thinking it would be great if my mommy would let me live with her again.

"We will probably age out of the system before that happens. I don't think they want us back. They haven't followed the court order and they don't stick with the visitation schedule," Jimmy said.

"My mom said she couldn't stand the sight of me after my daddy left because I look just like him. One day she dropped me off at the police station and told the officer she just couldn't do it and didn't want to be a mother anymore. I was five and will never forget that day," Brian said.

"What about your daddy?" I wanted to know.

"After he left, he just disappeared. No one knows where he is, including my mother," Brian informed.

"What about child support? He never paid child support?" Jack inquired.

"I don't know. I know my mom used to get a check in the mail, but I think that was a paycheck from her job," Brian said.

"Sounds to me like your mom was using your child support money as a paycheck. Maybe she does know where your dad is, but won't tell anyone so she can keep cashing those checks," Jack said.

"How long did you live with her after your dad left?" Angela asked.

"A few months, maybe," Brian said.

"Sounds like it was just long enough to be awarded child support along with receiving a couple of checks. You're lucky your mother gave you up rather than killing you for insurance money," Jack said, shrugging his shoulders and raising his eyebrows.

"Jack! That was an inappropriate comment," Angela chastised.

"Okay, well. Alex, what about you?" Jack said, turning the focus.

"I don't know and don't want to know," Alex said.

"You don't know what happened to your parents?" Angela asked Alex.

"Nope, maybe I was a baby, but I don't know," Alex theorized.

"How many homes have you been to?" Gwen asked me.

"My mommy just dumped me a other day. I went home with Officer Leigh, then came here. That's it," I told them.

"Wow, you got placed fast. Some of us spent a few days, up to a couple of weeks in the social worker's office," Angela said.

"I spent my first night at Officer Leigh's house. She's the one who picked me up from the building," I told them. "Then yesterday I met Janet Russell and she brought me here."

"If you have a cop on your side, you could easily get out of here. The cop might help get you placed in long term foster care awaiting adoption. Unfortunately, we aren't available for adoption. This is supposed to be our last stop before we go home as long as our parents do what they are told to do by the courts," Jimmy said.

"Maybe Mrs. Warren will let me call Officer Leigh," I wondered.

"Good luck with that. We aren't allowed to use the phone. If someone calls for us, like our social worker, she sits right with us and makes sure no one says anything about her," Angela told me.

"No. Officer Leigh said I can call her anytime I want and Mrs. Warren has to let me. I have her card with her number on it, so I just have to ask to use the phone," I told them.

"The only way you will be able to talk to Officer Leigh without Mrs. Warren knowing what you are telling her, is if the officer takes you away from the house," Jimmy said.

"No, just leave it alone. I don't want to move again. I have finally found my family and I will lose her if we are moved from here. Since most couples who are looking to adopt, want children under the age of five, we don't stand a chance," Angela said.

"Just go with the flow and hope for the best life you can have," Brian said. "You will be out before you know it, hopefully."

"Am I going to be here for a long time?" I asked.

"That all depends. If your social worker is able to find you a family soon, you won't be here long. I will tell you, the longer you are here, the easier it will be for Mrs. Warren to break your spirit and you will begin to become dependent on her and her instructions," Angela told me.

"I just want to be a kid. I don't want to clean the house like grown-ups," I said.

"Have you actually looked at the size of that lady? She can't do anything around her house, that's why we do it. Hell, she can barely breathe when she moves. I bet she is in there right now eating something," Alex said, rolling his eyes.

"What if I talk to Janet Russell? She is the one who put me here, maybe she can help get me out of here?" I expressed.

"If Mrs. Warren can break you down into complying with her demands, she will make up excuses to the social worker to keep you here," Gwen said. "On top of that, she won't even allow you to speak to the social worker alone. It's best to just let it go until you are moved."

"But how long will I have to wait? She had already hit me on my face twice. I don't want to know what happens if she is really mad," I informed them.

"She slapped you? When?" Jimmy said, balling his hands into fists.

"The first time was when she showed me which room I would be sleeping in. The second time was last night when she wouldn't let me eat dinner," I said.

"Why did she slap you? Do you know?" Brian wondered.

"I don't know. I just asked her some questions. Auntie May says asking questions is how we understand things," I explained.

"You can't ask her questions. She doesn't like being questioned," Jimmy informed.

"Please don't mention the Auntie May thing again. It's bad enough she has the boys call her 'Foster Mother', now we all have to call her 'Momma Warren'." Angela complained.

Seven

"Kids, come inside for lunch," Mrs. Warren yelled, from the back door.

We all stood up and ran toward the house, as fast as we could so we wouldn't get into trouble. Quietly, we stepped up to the table, the same as we had for breakfast and waited for instruction. Now that I knew everyone's name, I knew that Jack was the one who catered to Mrs. Warren. He pulled out her chair and he did special tasks for her.

Each one of the children had their own special tasks that were required by Mrs. Warren. I figured the reason Jack was basically her personal assistant was because he was the quietest of all the children, but I felt as though she was taking advantage of him.

"Girls, please. Angela and Gwen, you should be teaching Mackenzie what to do at meal times. Go, now," Mrs. Warren practically grunted, when she emerged from the kitchen with lunch and we were all standing around the table.

She snapped her fingers as if to rush us. The three of us scurried into the kitchen and repeated the process for table setting from breakfast. The boys were already sitting at the table when we came out and Mrs. Warren again said a prayer while we all held hands after Angela, Gwen and I were finally seated.

At lunch, I made sure to keep my face hovering over my plate and my fork positioned in my hand precisely located with the prongs either over the plate, or in my mouth. My face was so close to my plate, my chin was practically resting in my food. I was starving by that point in the day since I had missed dinner the night before because I made the mistake of saying I was tired and breakfast that morning was cut short when I made a mess. I was determined to actually eat a full meal.

"Mackenzie, were you taught to eat like a dog? Don't sit with your face so close to your plate, that's disgusting," Mrs. Warren said, shoveling food into her mouth.

"I'm sorry, I just don't want to make a mess," I answered.

"Are you talking back to me?" Mrs. Warren yelled, from her chair, slamming her fist on the table.

"No ma'am. I thought I was answering your question," I told her.

"I didn't ask you a question. I have all the answers and I'm smarter than you are. If I want you to talk, I'll beat it out of you, understand?" she scolded.

I nodded without speaking and continued to eat. My eyes roamed the table, scanning the other children. They were looking down at their food as they ate and Mrs. Warren snapped her fingers at me then pointed at my food when I looked at her. I looked down at my food like the other kids as we finished.

Once we were all done, the boys, along with Mrs. Warren, leaned back in their chairs as Angela, Gwen and I cleared the table. Once all the dishes were in the sink, the three of us rejoined the boys in a line up for chore instructions.

"Angela, you need to train Mackenzie so she knows what is expected from her daily. Mackenzie, you are going to be helping Angela with the dishes. Gwen, you are going to finish with this morning's laundry. Brian and Alex, the table and Jimmy and Jack, the floor. Go," Mrs. Warren instructed, from her chair at the table.

We all scrambled to get to our stations and complete the tasks we were given. I helped Angela with the dishes, while Gwen pulled the white table cloth from breakfast out of the dryer and folded it before putting it away. Brian wiped off the table after Alex sprayed the cleaner. Jimmy swept the floor and Jack mopped. When everything was done, we lined up and awaited further instruction.

"Jack, get the vacuum and go through the house. Jimmy, clean all the windows and mirrors. Angela, Gwen and Mackenzie, you three are going to clean the kitchen and do *all* the laundry. Go to each room and fetch the laundry baskets. Brian and Alex, you two are in charge of the bathrooms. That includes toilets, tubs and sinks. Let me know when each of you are done and I will check your work," Mrs. Warren instructed.

Angela, Gwen and I went down the hall and retrieved the dirty laundry from each room, other than mine since I had only been there for one day. We carried them out to the open laundry closet in the dining area. Gwen put the first load into the washer while Angela and I headed to the kitchen to get started. When Jack had finished the vacuuming, Mrs. Warren had moved from the chair at the table and into her chair in the living room.

"Okay Jack, go help your brother Jimmy with the windows and mirrors," Mrs. Warren told him.

The washer had stopped and Angela went over to move the clothes from the washer to the dryer while Gwen and I wiped down the lower cabinet doors.

When Jack and Jimmy finished, they put away their cleaning supplies and approached Mrs. Warren. They stood next to each other with their hands behind their backs, looking at the floor.

"Go help Brian and Alex. I'm sure the two of them are just fooling around in that bathroom and they still have to clean mine," she told them.

Jack and Jimmy headed down the hallway to the shared bathroom to assist the two younger boys. As soon as the three of us were finished in the kitchen, the buzzer went off on the dryer, so we put away the cleaning supplies and gathered the rags we used and headed to the laundry closet.

When the four boys had finally finished both bathrooms, they put away the cleaning supplies they had used and again, approached Mrs. Warren for further instructions.

"Great job boys. Glad to see some of you around here work hard to get things done in a timely manner. The four of you may go back out for yard time," Mrs. Warren told them.

The boys headed out the sliding glass door and toward the safe space, while Gwen, Angela and I continued folding laundry and taking it to each room, setting clothes on the bed to the person they belonged to.

As soon as the last stack of laundry had been delivered, Mrs. Warren allowed the three of us to join the boys outside. We ran off to the safe space in the corner of the yard, where the boys were waiting for us.

"I hate it here," Alex said, as soon as we were sitting in the same circle we had been in earlier in the day. "I'm tired of doing all the house cleaning here and her bathroom is gross."

"I can help get us all out of here. I need to make a call to Officer Leigh," I told them.

"I have been to several foster homes since my parents died. I'm done moving. I don't want to move anymore," Angela said. "All I have to do is wait a few more years and I will be out on my own."

"I don't like it here either, but I don't want to leave Angela. She is my sister; she is my family. We are forever," Gwen said.

"I plan to help Gwen get out of here, when I leave," Angela told us.

"I don't really care. Jack and I won't be here too much longer. When our parents are ready, we will go back with them," Jimmy said.

"Even if they don't want us back, it won't be long before we turn eighteen and are out on our own anyway," Jack said.

"Can you get *us* out of here?" Brian asked, referring to Alex and himself.

"If I tell Officer Leigh, or Janet Russell about how Mrs. Warren treats the children here, everyone can get out. I don't know what to say to only get two of you out," I told him.

"Please don't say anything," Angela pleaded.

"Fine, we will all just wait until we get old enough to be out on our own," I said, crossing my arms over my chest.

"That's not what I'm saying. I'm telling you that Mrs. Warren won't let you call Officer Leigh and if you blurt it out to your social worker, she will tell the social worker that you are exaggerating, then she will beat you after the social worker is gone. If you say anything or ask questions to Mrs. Warren, she will beat you until you comply with her rules. She is rougher on the girls than she is on the boys," Angela informed.

"I'm not scared of her. I will tell them right in front of her. I know how to pretend. I can pretend she is scary and tell Officer Leigh I don't feel safe," I told her.

"You don't understand. She is very manipulative and will be able to convince them that you are lying. I'm serious, you will be punished as soon as they leave. She will not let you call either one of them. If you were a boy, your punishment won't be as severe. Just let it go," Angela pleaded.

"Oh yeah, because being isolated in a closet for three days and only being fed once a day and having to go to the bathroom in a bucket for those three days isn't rough at all," Brian commented.

"Yes Brian, the boys get the naughty closet. We have already talked about it. I would rather be isolated in a closet, than beaten so badly that I had to throw out my clothes because we couldn't get the blood out," Angela said, raising her eyebrows and pursing her lips.

"This is *not* how children should be treated. Auntie May always said that children should be loved and not disciplined," I told them.

"It just seems like Mrs. Warren is looking for a free maid service and with the option of having foster children, she is being paid to house her maids," Jimmy stated.

"Look, you have only been here one day. When you get beat so badly you can barely move for a week, then you can get a say in whether or not we should stay or go," Angela told me, hugging Gwen.

Angela's comment gave me an idea. Although, I didn't know how bad it would be, I was willing to do something in order to help the other kids out of the horrible situation we were thrust into.

"So what do we do when we go back inside?" I asked.

"Whatever Mrs. Warren tells us to do," Alex said.

"Like always," Brian added.

"Since we did laundry today, we will have to put away our clothes," Gwen informed.

"That won't take long, so she will probably have us either stand in our bedroom doorways until she is ready for us to come out for dinner, or she will make us clean our rooms again, that doesn't take long either," Brian said.

"But it is T.V. night, so we will get to watch the television," Alex said.

"Oh yeah, for you guys, but the girls are ordered to do the dishes for most of the T.V. time. It's so unfair," Gwen complained.

"Let's go, time to come in for the night," Mrs. Warren called us, from the patio door.

When we had made it inside, we again all lined up by age, oldest first, our hands behind our backs and our heads down looking at the floor, awaiting instructions.

"You have laundry placed on your beds, except you, Mackenzie. You need to go put it away. Mackenzie, you can help the other girls with their laundry and Angela, make sure she chose the correct drawer in her dresser and that her clothing is put away neatly," Mrs. Warren ordered.

The seven of us headed to our rooms. I joined Angela and Gwen in their room and just waited for them to put away what little bit of clothes they had. Once they had finished, the three of us headed into my room.

"Which drawer did you choose?" Angela asked.

"I don't have a lot of stuff, so I put it in the small top drawer," I told her, opening the middle of the three top drawers.

"You can't do that. It doesn't matter how much stuff you have, it depends on your station here. You are new and therefore, you are in a lower station. You have to use the bottom drawer," Angela said, as she pulled my clothes out of the drawer and threw it on the floor.

I sat down and started refolding everything as Angela closed the small top drawer and opened the large bottom drawer. Angela and Gwen helped me place what little clothing I had, in a drawer that had more space than what I needed.

"Now what do we do?" I asked, after standing up.

"Now we wait in our doorway, like always. Mrs. Warren will check to make sure everything is in order before we are allowed to go out for dinner," Gwen said, leaving the room.

I followed Angela out to the hallway where the boys were already standing in their doorways. Angela joined Gwen in her doorway and I stayed in mine. All seven of us stared at the floor and waited.

When Mrs. Warren came to check our rooms, I made sure not to say anything so I would be able to eat dinner. Once she decided we were good, we all went out to eat. That time though, Angela, Gwen and I headed straight for the kitchen to collect place settings. We brought them in, set the table and sat down for the meal prayer.

Eight

Once we had finished dinner, Angela, Gwen and I walked around the table, picking up the plates, cutlery and napkins, taking them into the kitchen. Once the dishes were placed into the sink, we stepped out into the dining room with the boys for instruction.

"Alright boys, you are excused to go watch television," Mrs. Warren told them, before turning to us. "The three of you are going to clean the table, the floor, wash the dishes and clean the kitchen. Once you are done with that, then you can join us in the living room."

At that point I had had enough. I decided I didn't like being treated like her maid and in order to prove that she was abusive, I needed marks. I remembered what Angela had said about questioning Mrs. Warren and thought, for only a moment, about what I would say. Angela and Gwen turned and went straight to the kitchen, as the boys turned and headed toward the living room. Knowing I was testing the boundaries, I stood up straight and spoke with confidence.

"This isn't fair," I said, stomping my foot on the floor. "Why do you treat the girls different than the boys?" I asked.

"First of all, you don't question me. Secondly, the correct word is *differently* than the boys and last, I'm the adult around here and you are the child. You do whatever I tell you to do, or there will be consequences," she told me.

"You mean like when I didn't get to eat dinner yesterday because I said I was tired, or when I didn't get to finish my breakfast because like all kids, I made a mess, or are you referring to the two times you hit me on my face?" I said, with a sassy attitude.

"Are you looking for a beating?" Mrs. Warren said.

"Is that one of your consequences?" I asked.

"Go to your room, young lady."

"I want to call Officer Leigh."

"You do *not* tell me what to do. I tell you what to do, now go to your room."

At that point, all the other children had come into the dining room, where we were arguing and were watching it all unfold. I was refusing to back down. I decided that if I was going to live with random families, then I wanted to make sure they knew I wasn't going to back down from anyone.

"It's not my room. It's your room. I'm just being forced to stay in there," I told her.

"Mackenzie, stop," Angela said, from the opening of the kitchen.

"No, this is not right. I'm not going to stay here with someone who is going to treat us like maids. You're mean and no one likes it here. I want to call Officer Leigh to tell her I am not happy and have her find me a different house to go to," I argued.

"That's it, I'm done with your mouth," she said, grabbing my upper arm directly under my arm pit and squeezing as hard as she could.

She pulled me through the house toward the bedrooms. I struggled to keep my feet underneath me as I stumbled down the hall. She was squeezing my arm so tight I could feel my heart beating in my hand.

"Let me go! Don't touch me!" I yelled, as she practically dragged me.

"Shut your mouth," Mrs. Warren said, through clenched teeth, squeezing my arm harder.

Once we got to the room I was staying in, she shoved me toward the bed and pulled an extension cord out of her pocket. She straightened it out, then folded it in half.

I bounced off the edge of the mattress and fell to the floor. Once I was able to scramble to my feet, I tried to run passed her and out the doorway. She reached out and grabbed my hair, pulling me back toward the bed.

Mrs. Warren bent me over the side, pressed my face into the mattress with one hand and swung the cord with the other. The whooshing of the cord as it whipped back and forth, striking me on my back, arms and legs, caused the muscles in my body to tense. She just continued to whip my back and anything else she could reach, until she got tired.

"Please, stop! Owe, no! Stop, please," I screamed, pleading with her.

"You're going to learn little girl. If you continue to run your mouth, I will keep going. Shut up," she said, between swings of the cord.

Once I stopped yelling, she stopped beating me. I could hear her breathing heavily when she stopped. When she finally lifted her hand off my face, she didn't say anything, she just walked out. I slowly slid down off the edge of the bed and lowered myself to the floor Laying there on my side for a few moments, crying quietly. I didn't realize she would react so violently. I thought Angela was exaggerating.

"Angela, come tend to this," I heard Mrs. Warren say, as she walked down the hall.

A few minutes later, Angela and Gwen came in with first aid supplies. Angela helped me up off the floor and assisted me with carefully removing my pajamas. Some of the wounds on my legs were bleeding and some were just red and swollen. Angela picked up a spray bottle and sprayed something on the back of my legs that increased the pain.

I cried out in pain, as it felt as though Angela was rubbing sandpaper up and down both of my legs. "Owe, what is that?"

"Shhh, be quiet. She will come in here and hit all three of us. Please, don't yell out," Angela told me, as she dabbed at my wounds.

I leaned over the bed and placed both hands over my mouth in order to muffle the sound, which created a low grunting noise from my throat. When she stopped, I turned to see what she was going to do next.

Angela picked up a cotton ball and ointment. She squeezed the ointment onto the cotton ball and gently dabbed it on all of my wounds. She wrapped my legs in gauze and helped me put on a clean pajama set.

"Mackenzie, this is bad. You might need stitches on some of these cuts," Angela said, as she packed up the first aid kit. "Think of a plan to get out of here and let me know tomorrow during yard time. We will figure out how to get you out of here."

"Angela, I don't feel safe here. If she can do this to Mackenzie, I don't know what she would do to me. We need to all get out of this house. Please Mackenzie, I support you. Get us out of here," Gwen whispered, as Angela picked up the first aid supplies.

Angela nodded at me, as they both left the room and I stood up.

Within seconds, I heard Mrs. Warren scream at them. "What took you so damn long!"

"I'm sorry ma'am. We were taking care of Mackenzie," I heard Angela say.

"We also helped her change her clothes," I heard Gwen contribute.

"Is that back talk? You two know better than to speak to me like that." I heard the sound of one of the girls getting slapped. "Put that stuff away, shut up and sit down before the two of you get the same punishment," Mrs. Warren told them.

While the other children watched T.V. with our captor, I very carefully sat down on the bed. Pain radiated through my body with every slight movement I made.

As I rested for a moment, I thought about how we could escape. It wasn't like we would be able to just walk out the front door. If I would not be able to call Janet Russell or Officer Leigh, I knew we would have to sneak out.

Remembering the story Angela told me about Mia, where she had climbed out the window, I stood up and walked over to the window. I grabbed ahold of the cord and slowly pulled in order to retract the blinds, as well as, trying not to make too much noise.

I reached up and shifted the lock to the window in order to disengage. I hooked my fingers up under the lip at the bottom of the window and pushed it up. The seal around the window made a crackling sound as it pulled apart.

I stopped, and lowered the blinds, afraid Mrs. Warren heard the window open. I tip toed back over to the bed, trying not to put too much pressure on my legs. Leaning against the mattress face down, I lifted my legs up one by one to lay on my stomach. I waited for her to come into the room to see what I was doing.

I didn't have to wait long before Mrs. Warren came into the room. She walked into the bedroom and looked at several things before coming over and standing next to the bed.

"What did you do?" she asked.

"Nothing," I said, with my face pushed into the bed, facing the wall and not moving.

"Excuse me, but when I talk to you, I expect you to look at me."

"I can't move."

"Oh really? Do you want another beating?"

"I didn't do anything wrong," I pleaded, still not moving.

"This is ridiculous. You are going to do what I tell you to do and you will learn not to talk back," she said, striking me on the back with the extension cord, again.

I screamed into my pillow with each excruciating blow. Every muscle in my body was tight and tense awaiting each and every time the cord came into contact with my back. Mrs. Warren was hitting me so hard, my body bounced on the mattress. As soon as she stopped, I wiped the tears and snot off my face against the pillow.

I knew that Angela would come in to patch me up as soon as Mrs. Warren left. Once she came into the room, I would tell Angela my plan to sneak out the window and run away. Since I wouldn't know where to go if I went by myself, I would need the older kids to go with me. Plus, I would need help moving around.

"Angela, get Gwen and go in there. Fix her with the first aid so she can heal before the next social worker visit," Mrs. Warren yelled, once she was back out into the living room.

As soon as Angela came into the room, I heard her gasp.

Nine

I was in so much pain, I couldn't move at that point. I just cried.

"Shhh. I'm going to try and help you as much as I can. This shirt may have to be thrown away. I don't think we will be able to get the blood out," Angela said, as she very carefully pealed the back of my shirt up away from my skin.

I could feel the shirt separate from my skin as Angela tried to take my shirt off. There was sharp pain radiating through my entire body.

Angela was only able to get my shirt up to my arm pits. She sprayed my back the same as she did to my legs, which caused an influx of pain. I blacked out.

When I regained consciousness, Angela and Gwen were carefully moving me from the bed. When they placed me on the floor, I screamed out in pain.

"Shut her up back there. It should be quiet in this house. There is no need for all of this screeching," Betty yelled from the living room.

I did my best to stand up in front of Angela in order to position myself the best I could, so she could bandage me up. She began wrapping my back all the way around my front with gauze to hold it in place, then tucked the end into itself at my belly button.

"Please Angela. I can't get hit anymore. I need to call Officer Leigh and have her come get me, but I need help," I told her, as Gwen pulled another pajama set out of the dresser.

"She won't let you. There is no way to use the phone without her knowing," Angela said.

"I have the number for Officer Leigh. We just have to get out of this house and to a phone before Mrs. Warren even notices we are gone. Officer Leigh can pick us up," I told her, pulling Officer Leigh's business card out from under the pillow on the bed.

"How are we supposed to get out of the house?" Angela asked.

"Remember the story you said about Mia?" I inquired.

"You mean you want us to climb out the window?" Gwen said.

"Yes, I just need everyone to come too," I told them.

"I will have to find the time to tell the boys," Angela said.

"If Mrs. Warren comes back here and leaves y'all out there alone, you can tell the boys then what we are going to do."

"Okay, I will talk to the boys," Angela said, before leaving the room with Gwen.

I picked up the pajama set off the bed, where Gwen had placed it and moved slowly toward the dresser in order to retrieve a shirt to put on and change into jeans. My entire body was throbbing with each step I took. I whimpered and cried, hoping that Angela would be able to tell the boys the plan.

I pulled my pants up, wincing in pain as the denim slid over my leg wounds. Deciding I would wait to put my shirt on, I stuffed the shirt under my pillow and retrieved Officer Leigh's business card to slip into my back pocket. I shoved my bloody clothes into my bag to show Officer Leigh and placed the bag back under the bed.

After I stood back up, I bent over the mattress. Using all my strength, I pulled my legs up and laid down on the bed on my stomach like before, whimpering with each movement. Gently, I reached down and pulled the blanket up to my neck.

As I laid on the bed, my body began to relax. Starting at my neck and moving all the way through my muscles, I could feel my heart beat over my entire body. I was exhausted. I tried blinking my eyes slowly, so I could stay awake. Unfortunately, my exhaustion took over and I fell asleep.

I wasn't sure how long I had been asleep before I was awoken by the sound of Mrs. Warren's heavy breathing coming down the hall. She entered the room and stopped at the dresser, as if she were trying to catch her breath from the walk down the hallway. She stepped up next to my bed and hovered over me before speaking. I hoped that Angela and Gwen were talking to the boys while they were alone.

"Are you going to behave tomorrow?" she said, standing over me.

I didn't know if she would hit me again if I didn't answer, so I replied. "Yes ma'am," I said, laying on my stomach, still not facing her.

"Good, now get ready for bed," she told me, before leaving the room.

My entire body was throbbing and I couldn't turn over onto my back. I just waited and listened. When I heard the other children come down the hall, I moved as much as I could and waited to see the girls pass my doorway. They headed into the bathroom first.

I was sure Angela and Gwen were brushing their teeth and washing up for bed. I couldn't move my body in any way without pain. I groaned, trying to get their attention. It wasn't long before Gwen stepped up, next to the bed.

"Mackenzie, don't worry. Angela told the boys what you were planning and they are in. We will get out of here tonight," Gwen told me.

"Okay, tell her I said thank you" I told her, turning my head in order to look at her as she squatted next to the bed.

Angela entered the room and grabbed Gwen by her arm. She pulled her up into a standing position.

"I told the boys. Jimmy said he would take care of the rest," Angela said.

"Is everyone coming?" I asked.

"Yes, we are all coming with you," Gwen said, clapping her hands.

"Be quiet. You don't want her coming in here to yell at us. Gwen, go to the room. Mackenzie, we will come in here when we are sure there is enough time between bed checks to get away," Angela told me.

I slowly nodded, then turned my head back to face the wall. When Gwen and Angela left the room, I heard the knock on the wall to signal to the boys that it is their turn in the bathroom.

The four boys headed down the hallway and one entered the room I was in. I turned my head to see Jimmy crouched down next to the bed.

"Hey there. How are you doing?" Jimmy asked.

"Not good. I need to go to the doctor," I told him.

"We will get you a doctor when we get out of here," Jimmy said, standing up and walking over to the window.

He pushed the window up as far as he could without raising the blinds, then returned to the side of the bed. He smoothed his hand over the top of my head, then gently kissed my forehead before adjusting the blanket that was covering me.

Jimmy left my room just as the other boys rushed down the hallway, on the way to their bedrooms. I turned my head again to face the wall. I wanted to be in the same position I was in from the previous time Mrs. Warren had come into the room. I didn't want her to have any suspicion that the other kids had come into the room for any reason.

When Mrs. Warren yelled, "three minutes," I could hear rustling in the other bedrooms as if the others were discussing a plan.

When the six of them were settled in their rooms and it was quiet, we waited. We knew Betty Warren would be in shortly to check on us. I heard her heavy footsteps coming down the hallway and stop at my bedroom door first.

She didn't come into the bedroom, she just stood in the doorway. She made her way back down the hallway, going room to room and into the living room, where she had turned the volume up on the T.V.

A few moments later, I heard someone come into my room and stop next to my bed. When the person touched my arm, I turned my head to see Jimmy's face. He reached up and moved my hair out of my face.

"She is still up. It won't be long before she comes to check on us again. Once she goes to bed, we can get out of here. Just hang on a little longer, okay," he told me.

"How are we going to get away? I can barely move," I told him, tears soaking the pillow.

"Don't worry, Mackenzie. I will help you. If I have to, I will carry you. The next time I come back, we will all be here," Jimmy said, standing up, kissing me on the forehead and leaving the room.

I turned my head back to face the wall. He was right. It wasn't long before she came back and went room to room checking on the children. After she left the hallway, the television in the living room turned off.

After a few moments of silence, the other six kids entered the room. Angela pulled my covers down and helped me out of bed. I reached under the pillow and produced the shirt I had placed there earlier.

"Come on, Mackenzie. We don't have much time to get out of here," Angela told me, as I leaned back against the bed after standing.

"I feel dizzy," I told her, waiting for the room to stop spinning around me.

Jimmy and Jack pulled up the blinds and opened the window all the way. That time the window slid up quietly. Of course, I had already pealed apart the seal so it would make it easier for us to escape. Alex and Brian stood near Jimmy and Jack, while Angela and Gwen stayed with me over by the bed.

Once the window was fully open, Jack climbed out first, then Jimmy assisted Alex with climbing up onto the window sill and lowered him down to Jack. He repeated the process with Brian, then Gwen.

Jimmy walked over and assisted me with pulling my shirt on over my head. I pushed my arms through the sleeves, then leaned back against the mattress again.

"It's your turn, sweet girl," Jimmy told me, as he very carefully helped me walk over to the window.

Jimmy hooked his elbows up under my arm pits in order to assist me out the window. Angela reached down, lifted my legs up and placed them over the edge of the window as Jack reached up placing his hands around my waist. I was lowered down to Jack and he held on to me until my feet touched the ground.

The pain radiating through my body created an excruciating pull as I went through the open window and I let out a slight yelp.

I bit down on my lip as the other children shushed me. I stumbled to stand as Jack held onto my hips until I was stable enough to stand on my own. Gwen came over and hooked her elbow with mine, guiding me away from the open window. Jimmy helped Angela out the window, then he jumped out to join us.

As soon as Jimmy's feet touched the ground, he scooped me up into his arms and everyone started running. I knew the plan was to get as far away as possible, so we were running down the street as fast as we could go with my injuries. Once we were far enough to where we couldn't see the house, everyone stopped running.

"Can you walk?" Jimmy asked me.

"I think so," I said and he placed me down on my feet.

"Where are we going?" Angela asked, as we all walked down the street.

"We need to get to a phone," I said, pulling Officer Leigh's card out of my pocket.

Angela took the card from me and glanced at it as we continued passed all the houses on our way toward the main road.

"It's still early and some of these houses have their lights on. Maybe we could knock on someone's door and ask to use their phone," Brian suggested.

"Do you know any of the neighbors around here?" I asked.

"No, Mrs. Warren homeschool's us. We are only allowed to play in the backyard with each other. We aren't allowed to interact with the other neighborhood children," Alex said.

"Why?" I asked.

"Mrs. Warren says that kids that go to public schools are like feral children and they could be a bad influence on us. I personally think it's so we don't have anyone to tell that she is abusive," Angela said.

"What's feral children?" I asked, as we strolled down the street deciding which house to go to.

"It just means children that behave as though they were raised by wild animals," Jimmy told me.

"It wouldn't surprise me if none of these people even knew we were here. They probably don't know we exist," Gwen included.

"I think that we should go somewhere public. We could ask an employee to help us. It could seem more urgent and possibly safer that way," Jack suggested.

"How is going to a public place safer than going to someone's house? It could be less likely for her to find us inside a private home," Angela questioned.

"Think about it. We would be in a public place, with a lot of people around who would most likely want to help children. If we show an employee what that evil bitch did to Mackenzie, they might feel sorry for us and protect us just in case she shows up and tries to lie about how Kenzie was injured. The other grown-ups around will stop her from taking us and most likely tell her to wait for the police instead of just handing us over to the wicked witch of the west. If we go into someone's home and she shows up, there is only the homeowner there and they will just hand us over and accept her explanation just so they don't have to get involved," Jimmy explained.

"How many times have you run away from foster homes?" Angela wondered.

"When we were first taken into the foster care system, our social worker said it could be a few months before she could find a home that would take the two of us together. Jack vowed he would find me no matter how far apart we were and as many times as he had to. Of course, after the fourth time, our social worker finally found a home, where we could be placed together," Jimmy said, giving his brother a high five.

"Well, let's get out of this neighborhood before she realizes we are missing and comes looking for us," Angela said, linking her arm with Jack and leading the way.

Gwen and Brian linked their arms with mine. Alex walked behind with me with Jimmy. My body felt like it was on fire, but I kept going. I knew I needed professional medical attention and if we stayed with Betty Warren, I would not receive that.

Ten

We continued past private homes toward the main road. As we approached the main intersection, I dropped to my knees as my body gave up. Brian on one side of me and Gwen on the other, tried to lift me onto my feet so we could get to the corner.

"I can't go anymore," I cried, unable to get my feet underneath me.

Gwen and Brian tried to help me walk, but Jimmy scooped me up and carried me to where Jack and Angela had stopped.

"I don't know how much longer she can go. We need to get her help now," Jimmy said.

"We can go to that gas station, down there at the corner," Jack said, pointing toward a shopping center just a quarter of a mile down the street.

"What do we say when we get there?" Angela asked.

"We just tell them that we need help," Jimmy said, walking passed Jack and Angela, heading for the bright lights of the shopping center with me cradled in his arms.

"Well, we need to keep away from the road so people don't notice a bunch of kids walking down the street late at night," Jack said.

I turned my head, in order to see the others behind Jimmy. Brian, Alex and Gwen were ahead of Jack and Angela as they followed behind Jimmy.

We walked along the side of the road heading toward the gas station, staying closer to the drainage bayou trying not to draw attention to ourselves.

Once we had made it to the parking area of the shopping center, Jimmy put me down on my feet. The gas station was only fifty feet away, but at that point my entire body, from my head down to my toes, was throbbing. It felt as though I had been taken over by a celestial being and it was trying to get out.

I was having trouble keeping my eyes open and my head was bobbing, back and forth, as Jimmy tried helping me walk. It only took twenty feet before my body gave out. My legs wobbled underneath me until they stopped working. I fell to the ground onto my hands and knees, tears streaming down my face.

"Are you okay, Mackenzie?" Jimmy asked, dropping to his knees next to me.

"No, I'm not," I began, staring at the concrete, watching my tears create a puddle. "I'm scared to know where I might end up next. What if it's worse than being with Mrs. Warren?"

"Trust me sweet girl, nothing is worse than where we just escaped from," Jimmy said, standing up and extending his hand to me.

I turned over into a seated position, wiped my face with the bottom of my shirt and reached up, grabbing Jimmy's hand. As I stood up on my feet, Jimmy scooped me back up into his arms and carried me the final thirty feet to the front doors of the convenience store. As Jimmy laid me on the carpet in the middle of the floor, the others walked up to the counter where a young man stood reading a text book.

"Can I help you?" the clerk asked.

"We need to call someone. May we use your phone please?" Jack asked, with the most pathetic sounding tone, even I felt sorry for him.

"What happened to her?" the clerk wondered, asking about me.

"Our foster mother beat her for asking a question. She's only six and we ran away to get her help. Can you please call this officer so she can come get us?" Angela said, handing the clerk Officer Leigh's card.

He nodded, then turned to the phone and dialed the number. "I'm Dwane, by the way. If you need anything for her, let me know," he said, as he waited for the officer to answer on the other end of the line.

"Is there any way I could get some ice for her back?" Jimmy asked, as he rolled me up on my side.

"Of course. Let me get you a bag," Dwane told him.

Jimmy stroked his hand through my hair before standing and walking over to the counter. As Dwane spoke into the phone, he handed Jimmy a plastic bag and pointed toward the soda fountain machine where the ice dispenser was. Jimmy scooped ice into the bag, then came back over to me.

He placed the bag gently against my back and I started to close my eyes. Jimmy shook me slightly and I looked up at him.

"Don't go to sleep sweet girl. We need you to stay awake until you are looked at," Jimmy told me.

"I'm so tired," I said.

"Of course you are. Getting beat as badly as you did can take all the energy out of anyone," Angela said, sitting on the floor behind me and holding the bag for Jimmy.

"She is on her way. She said she will be bringing the police and an ambulance," Dwane said, after hanging up the phone.

"Thank you so much, sir. We really appreciate your help," Angela told him.

The other children sat around me as I lay on the floor. Every so often, Jimmy would nudge me if I started to fall asleep.

Once my back began feeling numb, I could hear sirens blaring, the high pitched squeal getting louder as it got closer. The first officer on the scene was Officer Leigh. She rushed through the doors of the convenience store and practically slid across the floor as she came down to get close to me.

"Oh sweetie, what happened?" Officer Leigh asked, as she stroked the hair on the top of my head.

"Betty Warren," was all I could muster the strength to say at that time.

"What happened to her?" she asked, looking up at Angela and Jimmy.

"She asked Mrs. Warren a question. Mrs. Warren doesn't like it when we talk or question her when she tells us to do things," Angela said.

"Mrs. Warren beat her with the extension cord she keeps in her pocket for whenever we get out of line. Mackenzie is badly bruised and cut up from the beating. We aren't sure how much blood she lost, but I've been trying to keep her awake," Jimmy told Officer Leigh.

"Let me see her wounds," Leigh requested from Jimmy.

Angela backed away from me with the ice bag in her hand. Jimmy reached over and tried to turn me onto my stomach. As he rolled me over, I felt a bolt of lightning surge through my body. With Officer Leigh by my side, I knew I was safe from danger, so I yelled out in pain.

"Sorry Kenzie," Jimmy apologized.

"There is blood all over the back of her shirt," Leigh said, once I was on my stomach. She lifted my shirt and asked, "who bandaged her up?"

"I did ma'am. Mrs. Warren requests that all wounds and marks made from her beatings must be tended to immediately so they don't leave permanent marks. That way we have no proof when the social worker comes for inspection," Angela informed her.

"I'm going to take care of this, Mackenzie. Don't you worry about anything," Leigh said, standing and heading for the door.

"Don't leave me," I yelled, as the door opened, tears streaming down my face.

"I will be right back," Leigh said, coming back over to me, kneeling down and stroking my hair. "Three officers just pulled up in their cruisers and I'm going to tell them where to find Betty Warren. The rest of you, stay with Mackenzie." Leigh stood up and again, headed for the door.

When she returned a few moments later, she was followed by two emergency medical technicians with a gurney. They laid a back board down on the floor next to me and rolled me over onto my back on the board.

My entire body felt as though thousands of needles were penetrating every muscle. I took a deep breath and yelled out in pain when they lifted the board up with me on it. Every movement hurt as they placed me on the gurney.

"Her wounds are on her back. You may have to lay her on her stomach in order to treat her," Officer Leigh informed the EMT's.

"They are also down the back of both her legs," Angela included, as I was wheeled out to the ambulance.

"How many times did that woman beat her?" Officer Leigh asked, as they all followed the gurney.

"At least twice, but Mrs. Warren will swing the extension cord until she is tired," Angela told her.

The EMT's stopped the gurney outside the backdoors to the ambulance. The two technicians stood on opposite sides of the gurney and one looked down at me.

"Mackenzie, I'm Greg and that's Benny. We are going to take care of you on the way to the hospital. Is it okay if we turn you over so we can see what happened to you?" the EMT to my right said.

"Yes, that's okay," I told him.

Greg wrapped his hands around the handles of the back board as Benny placed his hands on my left arm. As Greg pulled the back board out from underneath me, Benny gently turned me over onto my stomach.

"I don't want to go alone," I pleaded, as I was lifted into the back of the ambulance on the gurney.

"Angela, go with her. The rest of us will go in my car and meet you there," Leigh instructed.

Greg assisted Angela as she climbed up into the back of the ambulance with me and he followed up behind her. Benny closed the back doors and climbed up into the driver's seat of the ambulance. He drove to the hospital with the siren blaring.

"Are you the one who bandaged her up?" Greg asked Angela, as he cut my shirt open in the back.

"Yes sir. I have been bandaging up the kids Betty Warren has beat on for years. I told her not to ask questions, but the other kids were pleading for her to help get them out of the house because we are miserable there," Angela told him.

"Well, you did a great job taking care of her," he said, cutting the bandages.

Most of it was stuck to my skin from the blood that had dried. He tried to be careful, but I could feel blood dripping off my back from the wounds he reopened. As the air swept over my skin, the feeling of being scraped with sandpaper had returned.

"Is she going to be okay?" Angela asked.

"She's going to be just fine, thanks to you. All I am going to do is clean her up just a little bit and find out if any of the abrasions are deep enough to need stitches. Once we get her to the hospital, they are going to fix her up as good as new, then let her go home," Greg informed.

"But we don't have a home," Angela said, reaching out to hold my hand.

"I'm sure Officer Leigh and social services will take care of that," he reassured her.

"Hey Mackenzie, do you think Officer Leigh would let us stay with her for the night?" Angela asked.

"I'm sure if I ask, she will let all of us stay with her until they are able to find new homes for us," I told her.

Eleven

As the ambulance pulled up to the emergency entrance of the hospital, Benny, from the front seat, turned off the siren. Within a few moments, the back doors swung open and Benny was standing on the other side. He first assisted Angela out of the back of the ambulance before assisting with the gurney I was on.

As soon as the wheels touched the concrete below, Officer Leigh trailed behind Brian, Alex, Gwen, Jimmy and Jack, as they all ran toward me. All six of the other kids surrounded the gurney and held on to the sides as the EMT's wheeled me into the hospital. I reached out and touched Jimmy's hand.

"Alright kids, you're going to have to stay here in the waiting room while Mackenzie goes in for some tests. They are going to fix her up and help her so she isn't in so much pain. I'm sure that as soon as the doctor is done with her, we can go back to see her," Officer Leigh said.

Jimmy looked down at me and stroked my hair. "We'll be right here waiting for you. You're going to be just fine."

I was wheeled down a brightly lit hallway and into a room. The EMT's passed me over to a doctor and a couple of nurses. There was a small television like machine to the right side of a bed. The gurney was pushed up next to the bed and I was lifted off the gurney and placed onto the bed.

"What happened?" the doctor asked Greg.

"Six year old female, has multiple lacerations on her back and legs. She was beaten with an extension cord. Received minimal first aid by an eleven year old girl," Greg informed him.

"Thank you, we got it from here," one nurse informed Greg and Benny, as she stepped up to my right side and placed one of her hands on my arm.

"What's your name, sweetheart?" she asked.

"Mackenzie," I told her.

"Mackenzie, I'm going to give you something that is going to put you to sleep. When you wake up, the tests will be all over and the doctor will let you know when you can go home," the nurse told me, sticking a needle in the crook of my arm.

"I don't have a home," I said, as she taped the needle down to my arm and the other nurse put a clamp on my finger, which caused the little television to start beeping, before I fell asleep.

When I opened my eyes, Officer Leigh was sitting in a chair to the right of the bed I was in. Jimmy was sitting in a chair to the left of me, Angela, Jack and Gwen were sharing a sofa in the far corner of the room and Brian and Alex were trying to sit together in a chair next to the sofa. As I began to stir, they all stood up and surrounded the bed.

"How are you feeling, Mackenzie?" Officer Leigh asked.

"I'm okay ma'am," I told her.

"Do you think you would be willing to answer a couple of questions?"

"I guess so."

"Do you know why Betty Warren hit you?"

"Because I asked her why we weren't allowed to talk in the house and why the boys were able to relax after dinner, but the girls had to clean the house. I just questioned her rules and she became very angry with me," I told her.

"That's what Angela told me, but she didn't know why you were hit a second time."

"I couldn't move because my whole body hurt and she got mad because I wouldn't look at her when she was talking to me."

"You don't have to worry about Mrs. Warren anymore. The police have made a visit to her and it has been taken care of. Now, as for the seven of you, we are going to have to find you all new homes," Leigh told us.

"Is there any way we could stay with you for a little while?" I asked her.

"There are two reasons that is not going to work. First of all, you Miss Mackenzie, will be staying in the hospital until the doctor gets your test results back. As for the others, I don't have enough room in my home for everyone to stay with me. Also, my job is demanding and I can't give you children the kind of attention you deserve. I could possibly check on all of you at your new homes, but it is not advisable for foster children to stay with law enforcement considering the potential for dangerous situations," Officer Leigh responded, leaning back in her chair and crossing her arms over her chest.

"I understand. Can I get something to eat? I'm so hungry," I said, changing the subject.

"I will make sure you get food. Let me call in the nurse," she said, pressing a button on the side of the bed.

"Will I be able to finish it?" I asked.

"Of course you can," Officer Leigh said, confused.

"And even though I'm still kind of tired, I can eat?" I inquired.

"What the hell did this woman do to you in two days?"

"The first night I was there, after you left she made us clean everything so I was tired by dinner time, so she made me go to bed without dinner. Then the next morning, I accidentally dropped a piece of pancake on the table cloth, so she pulled me away from the table and made me sit in the corner while everyone else ate breakfast and she threw mine away," tears formed in my eyes as I spoke and I stared down at my hands.

"What kind of monster doesn't allow a child to eat. I am so sorry Mackenzie. I promise I didn't find anything in her background check that implied abuse of any kind," Leigh said, stroking my hair.

"Of course not. No one would dare say anything in fear of the repercussions," Angela told her.

A nurse came into the room and pressed the same button on the bed that Officer Leigh had pressed to call her in there. She checked the machines I was hooked up to before she spoke to me.

"Did you need help with something?" the nurse asked, as she looked at the others in the room with me.

"Is there any way we can get her something to eat?" Jimmy spoke up.

"I suppose we can get something up here for her. As the anesthesia wears off, she will become hungry," the nurse said, checking my vitals before she walked out of the room.

"So what is going to happen with the rest of us?" Angela asked Officer Leigh.

"Janet Russell said that since the hospital would allow us to stay in the room with Mackenzie, she would allow you all to stay here until she is released by the doctor, but after that, Janet says you will be split up and placed in separate homes," Leigh informed.

"I knew it. I knew this was a bad idea. I told you to just shut your mouth and wait it out and you would go live with another family, but no. You just had to open your mouth and question her. Now Gwen and I are going to be separated," Angela complained.

"Wait a minute, are you and Gwen siblings?" Leigh asked Angela.

"No, but she is my foster sister and I don't want to lose her," Angela told Leigh.

"Let me see what I can do about keeping you two together," Leigh said, leaving the room.

"Are we going to stay together, Jack?" Jimmy asked his brother.

"Of course we are, stupid. We are siblings and our parents haven't lost custody of us, yet," Jack said.

Brian and Alex looked at each other and mumbled in winey voices as if to mock the others.

"What's going to happen to us?" Brian wined.

"Oh no, a new home," Alex imitated, bending his arms and waving his hands around at his shoulders.

"Boo hoo," Brian faked emotion, miming rubbing his eyes with his fists.

"Waah," Alex copied.

"All right you two. That's enough," Angela scolded.

Brian and Alex laughed as they slapped their right hands together in a high five. The two boys fell into the chair they were previously sharing and continued to quietly make fake crying sounds to one another. Angela rolled her eyes at the boys as she and Gwen returned to the plastic like sofa. Gwen leaned into Angela and Angela wrapped her arms around her foster sister.

"Okay," Officer Leigh began, as she re-entered the room, followed by someone carrying a food tray for me. "I spoke to Janet Russell and you all have been taken care of. Jack and Jimmy, the two of you are going to a foster home that is within walking distance from where your parents are living now. The two of you will be able to have regular visits with them every Wednesday after school and all day Saturday," Leigh began.

"Of course, that is only if they want to visit with us," Jack said.

"Janet has already contacted your parents and that is what they agreed to," Leigh said.

"What about the people we are going to be staying with? Anything that we should know about?" Jimmy asked.

"The couple has fostered children for the past thirty five years. All of their children are always un-adoptable due to their parents only temporarily having their rights taken away. Most of the children live with them until they grow up and move out on their own. If you are there during a holiday, you will probably meet about twenty five of their foster children who's parents never regained custody," Leigh explained.

"Good to know that at least we will have a family even if it doesn't include our real parents," Jack commented.

"Okay, moving on. Gwen and Angela, you two are going to the home of a nice couple who would like to adopt, but don't want to start at the baby stage. They are in their forties and have been unable to conceive for the past ten years. They said they had hoped to have at least two children by now, but they don't want them under the age of five. The two of you can be sisters," Officer Leigh reassured them.

"Thank you, Officer," Angela said, hugging Gwen closer to her.

"Brian and Alex, Janet said the two of you will be going to different homes, but in the same neighborhood. You will still get to play together if you choose," Officer Leigh told them.

"Are we going to school, or is it going to be the same homeschooling bull shit like Mrs. Warren?" Brian inquired.

"Brian, watch your mouth," Angela scolded.

"Sorry, but it's true," Brian said, shrugging.

"You both will be in the same school district and yes, both families will send you two to school," Officer Leigh said, sighing and shaking her head.

"Mackenzie, Janet has decided to send you to a foster care facility for now to keep an eye on you. A doctor will visit with you daily in order to keep an eye on your wounds, until you are healed. There are a lot of other children there and there is more than one caretaker," Leigh informed.

"Does that mean Mackenzie is going to an orphanage?" Gwen asked.

"It's more like a boarding school," Leigh explained. "There will be classes for her to attend during the day and she will be sleeping in a dorm with only girls."

Gwen let out a loud yawn and Angela moved over on the sofa. Gwen leaned toward Angela and laid her head in Angela's lap. Jack walked over to the sofa, lifted up Gwen's legs and sat down, placing her legs over his lap.

"Y'all should really get some sleep. Janet will be here as soon as we get the order that Mackenzie is going to be released. She will pick y'all up and take you to your new homes. Mackenzie, I will be taking you to the facility as soon as I sign the release papers," Leigh said.

Brian and Alex did their best to try to get comfortable together in one chair. Jimmy stayed next to the bed at my side, holding my hand.

"Hey, why don't one of you guys take this chair over here," Jimmy said, motioning to the chair he had previously occupied.

Both Brian and Alex ran for the chair. With Brian being slightly older and a little taller, he made it to the chair first. Both boys giggled as Brian settled into the chair next to me and Alex skipped back over to the chair across the room.

"Apparently when children aren't allowed to act like children for a while, I guess the sillies come out when they are given the right to be children again," Officer Leigh said, laughing at the boys antics.

"Is it okay if I lay next to you?" Jimmy asked me.

I nodded and very carefully slid my body over to give him room. He climbed up onto the bed next to me and held my hand.

I looked around the room at the six children I would probably never see again, once we were all separated. I was glad that I was able to get them out of that house, but I was sad that I was going to be alone without any friends.

Twelve

The next morning, other than Officer Leigh, I was the first to wake up. Jimmy was still in the bed next to me and Leigh was in the chair on the other side.

"How are you feeling this morning?" Leigh whispered.

"My whole body hurts. I can feel my heart beating all over," I told her.

Jimmy began to stir next to me. As he moved, he put slight pressure against my side and I whimpered, feeling a sharp pain radiate through my body. He opened his eyes and immediately rolled off the side of the bed.

"I'm sorry, sweet girl. Did I hurt you?" he asked, standing next to me, holding my hand.

"It's okay," I told him, tears rolling down my face.

When the others had woke up, a nurse entered the room with food for everyone. Angela, Gwen and Jack did their best to eat with the trays on their lap, sitting on the sofa. Brian and Alex were still sitting in separate chairs with their trays on their laps as well. Jimmy decided to stand next to the bed and share the rolling table with me.

By the time we had finished, Officer Leigh stood, took the food trays and left the room. The others gathered around the bed and began asking me questions.

"How are you feeling this morning?" Angela asked, as she stood at the foot of the bed.

"Still a little sore, but it's okay. I promise, I will be okay," I told them.

"I hope so. Make sure you keep that sassy attitude. You're going to need it, for the rest of your life," Jimmy said, grabbing my hand.

"You went off on that bitch," Brian said, smiling.

"Brian, why do you have to say bad words?" Gwen asked.

"What? Mrs. Warren was a bitch," Alex said.

"Well yes, but you don't have to use that word," Angela told them.

When Officer Leigh re-entered the room, she was holding one of the outfits she had bought for me. The doctor was directly behind her as Janet Russell followed in last. The doctor was holding a medical chart and stood at the foot of the bed between Angela and Gwen.

"You are one lucky little lady. No internal injuries, just a lot of cuts and bruises," the doctor announced. "I'm going to keep you one more day just for observation and you can leave tomorrow morning."

"Thank you doctor," Officer Leigh said, shaking the doctor's hand.

As soon as the doctor left, the other kids cheered. Angela and Gwen hugged each other and Jack wrapped his arms around the both of them together. Brian and

Alex chest bumped each other and Jimmy cradled my hand between both of his.

Janet waved her hands, in an attempt to calm everyone, as she spoke to the group. "Okay kids, Officer Leigh is going to take care of Makenzie. Tell her good bye. I'm going to drop all of you off at your new homes."

"Hey kid, maybe I'll see you again someday," Angela said, gently hugging me. "Thanks for saving us."

"You're my hero," Gwen told me.

"You did what none of us had the guts to do," Jack said, patting my shoulder.

"Thank you, Mackenzie," Alex said.

"Thank you for getting us out of that house," Brian told me.

"I appreciate what you did for us," Jimmy said, running his fingers through my hair.

"I appreciate you helping me. Thank you for what you did for me," I told him, as he bent down and kissed my forehead.

Jimmy patted me on the shoulder as Janet led the other kids out of the room. Jimmy strolled out behind them and I watched them all walk out of my life.

"Alright sweetie, let's get you dressed," Leigh said, once we were alone in the room.

"What about the rest of my stuff? It was all left at Mrs. Warren's house when we ran away," I asked Officer Leigh.

"Janet and I got everyone's things. There isn't a single item left at that house to indicate that children ever lived there," Leigh told me.

"You got my bag and everything?"

"Sure do. It's in my car. By the way, I saw the bloody clothes in your bag."

"I put them in there so you would see it," I told her, looking down at my hands.

"I'm glad you did," Officer Leigh said, setting my outfit down on the bed for me to get dressed.

Officer Leigh helped me climb down off the bed and pulled the curtain closed to block the view if some-one were to enter the room. I held onto the edge of the bed rail, trying to stand on my own. As I stood there, my legs began to shake and I felt weak. My whole body was tense and throbbing. Every movement I made wore me out.

"Are you okay?" Leigh asked, helping me to sit on the chair she had occupied.

"My legs don't work right," I told her.

"Let me help you," she suggested.

Officer Leigh untied the strings on the back of the hospital gown, then turned to pick up my shirt. She helped me pull my arms out of the gown and I held it under my arm pits to basically keep myself covered.

"How bad is my back?" I asked Leigh.

"I don't know sweetie. There is a bandage covering your wounds," she told me.

She pushed my shirt over my head and I lifted my arms up, one at a time, slipping them through the sleeves. I had to take a break and gently leaned back against the chair. I took a couple of deep breaths, as Leigh picked up my pants.

"Just relax. If you want, we can wait to put your pants on until tomorrow before you leave," Leigh sug-gested.

"That might be better. I just want to lay down," I told her.

I placed my hands on my knees in order to catch my breath. My back felt like thousands of needles were being pressed into my muscles and my spine. I leaned forward, in order to take the pressure off my back.

"I got you honey," Officer Leigh said, scooping me up into her arms.

She placed me down, on my back, on the bed with the hospital gown draped over my lower half. Tears were rolling down my cheeks as pain radiated through my body. I whimpered as I tried to turn onto my side.

"I'm going to be okay," I whispered, more to myself than to Leigh.

"That's right sweetie. You're going to be okay," Leigh said, placing my pants on the edge of the bed and pulling the blanket up over me.

As I laid on my side, crying from the pain, a nurse entered the room. She was pushing a cart with several first aid supplies on top.

"How are you doing?" the nurse asked.

"I'm going to be okay," I told her.

"Yes, you are. I'm just going to check your back and the back of your legs to make sure you are healing and bandage you back up. Is that okay?" the nurse informed.

I nodded and rolled over, so I was laying on my stomach. I rubbed my face into the pillow, trying to wipe off the tears. Officer Leigh sat down and watched as the nurse lifted my shirt up in order to access the wounds on my back.

"Are you doing okay?" the nurse asked, pulling up the bandages off my back.

"Uh huh," I said, grunting the sound out of my mouth.

"Well, your wounds are looking good. I'm just going to spray an antiseptic on your back to keep from getting an infection. It might hurt just a little at first, but it should soothe your pain," the nurse informed.

"It's okay. I can take it," I told her, gripping tightly onto the blanket as I felt the sting of the spray.

Officer Leigh reached up and grabbed one of my hands. I cried out in pain as the nurse dabbed a cloth over my back. Officer Leigh stood up and ran her fingers through my hair, in an attempt to make me feel better.

Thirteen

The next morning, the doctor entered the room with a clipboard. He handed it to Officer Leigh, then stepped up next to the bed.

"Good morning Mackenzie. How are you feeling today?" he asked.

"A little better," I told him.

"She has been laying on her side all night. I helped her to the bathroom once in the middle of the night, but she was able to walk back to the bed on her own. I did, however, have to help her back up into the bed," Leigh informed him.

"That's because when I tried to climb up, it felt like a monster with sharp nails was scratching my back," I said.

"Well, let me look at your back and see how it is healing," he said.

I rolled over onto my stomach as he lifted my shirt up. He pealed the bandages back and pressed his finger against my back around the abrasions.

"Owe," I complained, as he pressed down on a tender spot on my back.

"There is still some bruising and redness around the cuts, but the skin is healing nicely. I will have the nurse come in to clean and re-bandage your back. Other than that, Officer Leigh has just signed your release papers and you are free to go," the doctor said, taking the clipboard back from Leigh and leaving the room.

"Are you happy you get to leave today?" Leigh asked.

"I'm happy just to be able to go outside, but I would be happier to go see Auntie May," I told her.

"Hopefully we can find her soon," Leigh said.

After a few moments, the nurse came into the room with the first aid cart. I wasn't looking forward to the antiseptic spray, but I was looking forward to being able to finally put pants on.

For a little while after the nurse had re-bandaged my back and legs, I laid still. I waited for her to leave the room and Officer Leigh to come over and help me turn to my side like she had done the day before.

Once I was on my side, Officer Leigh brought the chair she was sitting on over to the side of the bed, so I could stand up out of the bed. I sat down on the chair and she helped me put on my pants. She placed the waistband over my feet and pushed up each pant leg until my feet peeked out at the end. I stood up and pulled my pants up the rest of the way and fastened them.

"Are you ready to go?" Officer Leigh asked.

"I guess so," I told her, shrugging.

We left the hospital and headed out to Officer Leigh's car. As she drove me to the foster care facility, I looked out the window and watched the trees go by.

"You will have a doctor visit you daily to check on your back and legs in order to make sure you are healing," Leigh informed.

"Is the doctor going to spray the stuff on me that makes it sting?" I asked.

"Maybe, but the doctor will decide the best first aid to be sure your wounds heal."

As Officer Leigh pulled off the main road and drove down the long winding private road to the facility, I observed the wide building, which was only four stories high. Officer Leigh began going into details about the history of the facility as if I were taking a tour of a museum, but in my six year old mind, I didn't quite understand most of what she said.

"The facility sits on six hundred acres. The ten thousand square foot building was built thirty years ago originally as a boarding school for pregnant teens and unwed mothers. It was a place for them to go until their babies were born. Ninety percent of those women would give their children up for adoption and those children would be adopted from this facility.

"The rooms have been remodeled now. There are still rooms for pregnant teens, but most of those teens are already in the foster care system. You will be staying with girls your own age," Leigh told me.

"There aren't any grown-ups here?" I asked.

"There are, but here, once you turn six years old, you are taught life skills in order to take care of yourself. You will have an orientation that will tell you everything you need to know. Are you ready to go inside?" she asked, as she pulled up to the front of the building.

"Yes ma'am."

There were five concrete steps up to a large concrete porch. On the concrete porch there were several round tables with four chairs at each one. The steps were only a few feet from the front doors. The double front doors were a mashed pea color and the building was built with brown brick.

Leigh touched my knee, with a soft, reassuring touch, before she turned off the car and got out. She came around the vehicle and opened the back door for me. After she retrieved my bag from the trunk of the car, she extended her hand. I grabbed her hand as leverage to stand up. As we walked toward the front steps, a woman with black curly hair, wearing a skirt suit, emerged from the front doors.

"Welcome Mackenzie. I hope you will be happy here. I'm Susan Riley. Please, feel free to come to me with any questions, or concerns you may have," the well dressed woman said.

"Isn't that great, Mackenzie? You can ask all the questions you want," Leigh said, nudging me.

"I think I will keep my questions to myself for a while," I said, hiding behind Leigh.

"Well, whenever you are ready to talk, someone will be there to listen to you," Susan Riley told me. "Let's go inside for orientation."

We walked toward the steps and Officer Leigh traipsed up in order to shake her hand. Susan led Leigh into the facility as I lagged behind. My legs felt like lead weights as I lifted each one slowly onto each step. They stood in the foyer waiting for me to catch up to them. I stopped just outside and peered in the open doorway.

"Come on in Mackenzie," Leigh urged, patting her leg.

I stepped inside, walked up to her and wrapped my arms around her thigh. I watched as children of all ages walked passed from all around us. They were in groups and they were talking and laughing. As I watched everyone seemingly having a good time, I loosened my grip on Leigh's leg and felt more comfortable about being there.

There was a hallway to the left and a hallway to the right. Both hallways turned around a corner, so I wasn't able to see where they ended. The tiles on the floor indicated division. There was a trail from the front doors, which divided a large open area, that led toward the back. Each side of the trail was set up like two separate living rooms. Neither room had a television, but I was okay with that.

"You might have to give her some time before she opens up, or trusts a grown up. She has had a rough week and her caretakers are the ones who have made it rough for her," Leigh told Susan.

"Hey Gertrude, could you show Mackenzie to her room so she can put her stuff away," Susan asked another lady, as she approached us.

"Hello Mackenzie, I'm Gertrude. Everyone around here calls me Miss Gertie. I'm going to show you the dorms and which room you'll be staying in," she said, presenting her hand to me.

Gertrude was a tall lanky woman. She wore a long, navy blue dress with a floral pattern and a yellow cardigan draped over her shoulders.

I hid behind Leigh and refused to hold Gertrude's hand. Leigh placed her hands on my shoulders and knelt down to get eye level with me.

"Mackenzie, you are going to be staying here for a while. This is a safe place, I promise. Look, if it will make you feel better, I will come check on you tomorrow while I'm out on patrol," she told me.

I nodded and fell into her for a hug. I started to cry, not knowing how safe I really was. When she wrapped her arms around me, she barely touched me so she wouldn't hurt me. I pulled away from Leigh, but still refused to take Gertrude's hand. Leigh nodded to Gertrude as she retracted her hand, then led me down the hallway to the left of the front door.

"This facility has been here for thirty years," Gertrude told me, as we walked up the stairs at the end of the hallway. "For the past ten years it has housed thousands of children in the foster care system and kept them safe. The girls are housed on this side and the boys are on the other side. You will be staying in a room with seven other girls. Five of them are six, just like you, one is twelve and the oldest is fifteen. She will be the one you go to first if you have any problems."

She took me up to the third floor and opened the door between the stairs and the hallway. As we walked down the hall, passed closed doors, the first thing I thought about was the fact that each room had a door, unlike the rooms at Betty Warren's house.

Miss Gertie stopped in front of the fourth room from the stairs and opened the door. I immediately began screaming and hyperventilating.

"No! I can't go in there. I won't go in there. You can't make me," I screamed, as I backed away from the room and pressed my back against the opposite wall.

I heard footsteps running up the stairs. Officer Leigh came barging through the door into the hallway, as I sat down in front of the wall, staring at the open bedroom door. Leigh sat down on the floor in front of me and ran her fingers through my hair.

"What happened?" Leigh asked Gertrude.

"I don't know. I opened the door to her assigned room and she started screaming," Gertrude answered, as Susan came through the door and into the hallway with us.

"Mackenzie, what happened?" Leigh asked me.

"Fourth room, fourth room," I said.

"What does that mean?" Gertrude asked.

"She stayed in the fourth room at her last foster home where the foster mother there hurt her, in that room," Leigh explained to Gertrude and Susan, before focusing back on me. "Mackenzie, we can find you another room."

"The room mother in this room is sensitive to abused children. This room is the best placement for her," Susan informed.

Trembling, I stood up and rubbed my face. I took a couple of deep breaths, then wiped my face with the bottom of my shirt. Taking a step forward toward the room, my knees buckled under me and I fell to the floor.

"Are you okay, Mackenzie?" Gertrude asked, sitting on the floor next to Leigh.

I scooted closer to Officer Leigh and laid my head down on her leg, crying. Officer Leigh ran her fingers through my hair.

"Susan, are you sure we can't move her to another room? This could be detrimental to her. She is associating the fourth room with a traumatic experience in her life," Officer Leigh requested.

"Mackenzie, there is someone who lives in this room that is able to help you to recover from what happened to you. She has gone through a similar situation and I promise, she is the best person to help you," Gertrude informed.

I sat up and touched Officer Leigh's hand. Leigh smoothed her other hand through my hair. Gently moving down my face and putting her hand under my chin, she gently pushed in order to lift my head.

"Can you at least try this, or do you want me to contact Mrs. Russell?" Leigh asked.

"I can do this. It's okay," I told Leigh.

"Are you sure?" she asked.

"Yes, it's like Jimmy told me, I have to stay strong," I said, standing up and picking my bag up off the floor.

Leigh pulled herself up onto her knees in front of me. She placed her hands on my shoulders and looked into my eyes.

"Are you sure you're okay with this?" Leigh asked me.

"Yeah, I can do this," I said, taking a deep breath and turning toward Gertrude, who had stood up and moved into the open doorway of the fourth room.

I again stepped toward the room, stopped in the doorway and took a deep breath before turning and waving good bye to Officer Leigh.

"I will stop in and check on you tomorrow, okay," Leigh told me.

"Okay, see you tomorrow," I told her, then stepped into the room.

Fourteen

There were three sets of bunk beds, one single bed and one double bed. The third set of bunk beds had only one bunk that was visibly not being slept in. I walked over and placed my bag on the floor in front of the bed, then sat down next to it.

"You can sit on the bed. The other girls will join you shortly. Are you sure you're going to be okay in here?" Gertrude asked me.

"After a while, I will be okay. Who are the other girls that are going to be staying with me in this room?" I asked, picking myself up and sitting on the bed.

"Well, the two girls in the first two bunks by the door, is Diane on the bottom and Jane on the top. Next to those bunks, you have Rachel on the bottom next to you and Eliza on the top. In the bed above you is Joyce. In the single bed is twelve year old Shirley. She will show you to your classes and help you with any class-work you might need help with.

"In the double bed is fifteen year old Prudence. She is your room mother. She is the one you go to for any-thing. If she feels that you would benefit from talking to a grown-up, she will set up a meeting with me and we can talk about what might be bothering you," Gertrude told me.

Just then, all the girls came rushing in the room, laughing. Once they noticed the two of us were in the room, they each greeted Gertrude with an embrace.

"Miss Gertie, who's our new roommate?" one girl asked.

"Girls, this is Mackenzie. Mackenzie, this is Diane, Jane, Rachel, Eliza, Joyce, Shirley and Prudence," Gertrude introduced the girls, as they lined up and stood in front of their beds.

Each one of them walked over and surrounded me as I sat on my assigned bed. They sat down on the bed next to me as well as on Rachel's bed in front of me. As they stared at me quietly, I didn't know what they wanted me to say, so I sat there, nervously smiling at each one of them.

Diane had short curly black hair and green eyes. She had a sad look on her face, which I wasn't sure if she was sad for me, or if she was hurt as well and it was more sympathetic.

Jane had long blond hair and blue eyes. She looked excited to have a new roommate. Her legs were swinging over the edge of the bed and she was bouncing.

Rachel's hair was covered with a hijab, but her eyes were brown. She sat on the bed next to me and held my hand in a comforting way. It was actually helping me relax a little bit due to the fact that I was feeling incredibly overwhelmed with moving several times in the past few days. I felt as though we could be best friends.

Eliza had long, thick, dark brown hair and brown eyes. She wouldn't look directly at me, so I just assumed she was shy.

Joyce was brushing her shoulder length, flaming red hair. She pretty much seemed indifferent toward me, but I figured she would be different once she got to know me.

Shirley was a very thin girl. Her very short blonde hair was so thin, I could see her scalp through the parts in her hair. Every time she reached up and ran her fingers through her hair, several strands would fall to the floor.

"Mackenzie, we are here to help you adjust to your new life. If you have any questions or concerns, please ask any of us. If you need a hug, or just want some loving attention, I'm here for you. I am what they call the room mother," Prudence told me.

Even though Prudence was fifteen, she wore her brown hair in pigtails. The tips of her hair were more of a golden blonde compared to the chestnut color of the rest of her hair. She had a very athletic body type.

"I'm going to let you girls get to know each other. Make sure you tell Mackenzie what the schedule is like around here, so she knows what is expected from her. Also Prudence, show her around the facility so she doesn't get lost on her first day and make sure you run her through the basic orientation," Gertrude said, before leaving the room.

"Okay girls, give her some space," Prudence said, shooing the others over to her bed.

The six other girls gathered on Prudence's double bed, as she sat down on Rachel's bed. She was sitting in front of me with her hands on her knees.

"Do you have any questions for me before we start the tour?" Prudence asked.

"Do they hit us here?" I asked, after a few seconds of silence.

"Oh, no sweetie. You will never have to worry about that. Mrs. Riley is only visible in the hallway when new kids come in, or if someone is here to look at the kids for adoption. As for Miss Gertie, she's like our therapist. If we are having trouble expressing our emotions, she will try to find out what's going on. I will tell you though, if you do talk to Miss Gertie, you will be emotionally drained for at least a day afterward. She will have you excused from classes the next day and will bring your meals and classwork to you, here in the room. All day she will check on you and make sure you are processing those feelings properly," Prudence reassured me.

"It's really nice here. Better than foster homes. You know exactly when you are going to be fed and exactly when to go to bed. This is my third home and I never want to leave. I am studying to be a teacher here so when I age out of the system, I get to stay," Shirley told me, from Prudence's bed.

"I don't want to stay any longer than I have to. I want a family with a mommy and daddy," Joyce said, flipping her hair.

"I don't care either way. My real mommy took me to a hotel and left me there. Then the first foster home I went to, the lady beat me. I have to see the doctor tomorrow to make sure my cuts are healing. I don't know if I really want a mommy," I told them.

"What about your daddy?" Jane asked.

"I don't know him," I informed.

"I will make sure you feel safe while you are here. Each one of us is here for a reason and we each stay here for different lengths of time. Those of us who are about to age out of the system, usually come here because none of the foster homes want a kid older than thirteen and we will be here until we find a job and are able to live on our own. The younger kids are here for one of two reasons. Number one, to get acclimated to the foster care system, or number two, because you were abused at your last foster home," Prudence informed.

"Well, I'm both of those," I said.

"Why both?" Eliza asked.

"My mommy left me in a hotel on Saturday. That night I was able to stay with the police officer who picked me up. On Sunday I went to stay with a lady named Betty Warren. Monday night and all of Tuesday and Tuesday night I was in the hospital and now, here I am," I said, laying out my week for them.

"Oh my goodness. It's only Wednesday. You're telling us this just happened to you?" Shirley asked.

"Yep," was all I said.

"Well, let's get you unpacked and I'll show you around the facility," Prudence told me.

"Which drawer can I use? I don't want to get in trouble for using the wrong drawer," I said.

"Don't worry sweetie. Each one of us is assigned a drawer. Your name is actually on the drawer so there is no confusion, but if you were to accidentally put your clothes in a different drawer, or take out someone else's clothes, you're not going to get in trouble," Prudence told me, putting her arm around my shoulders.

I nodded and stood up walking over to the dresser. I spotted a door to the left of the dresser and thought it could be a closet. I opened the drawer marked with my name, then walked over and retrieved my bag. When I began pulling my clothes out of the bag Rachel came over to help me.

"This here is our bathroom. It only has a toilet and a sink for us during the night, otherwise there is a communal bathroom with showers down the hall. I will take you there once you have put your clothes away," Prudence said, referring to the door I thought was a closet as if she could read my mind.

Once Rachel and I had finished putting away my clothes, Rachel folded my bag flat, then slid it under my bed. Prudence opened the door to the bathroom and I peeked in just to satisfy her. I had seen plenty of bathrooms before, but since she opened the door to show me, I looked.

"Okay, let's go around and I will show you the facility. Girls, go ahead and get ready to go down for dinner. You have about an hour before you have to be down in the dining hall. I will meet y'all down there when I am done showing Mackenzie around," Prudence directed the other girls.

"May I go with you?" Rachel asked Prudence.

"Is there anything you need to do before dinner?" Prudence asked her.

"No ma'am, I promise," Rachel reassured her.

"Okay, Mackenzie are you okay with that?" Prudence asked me.

"Yeah, that's okay," I told her.

"Alright then, let's go," Prudence said, leading Rachel and me out of the room.

Once we were out in the hallway, Rachel grabbed my hand as we walked in the opposite direction from the stairs.

Fifteen

After a month had passed since I had arrived at the facility, the school year started. My wounds had almost completely healed and I was moving normal again. Every day was scheduled like clockwork. Everyone was required to get up by six in the morning and be ready for breakfast by seven.

The classes we took during the day were basic. I really liked the fact that we were placed in a class based on our learning ability and not by age. Miss Gertie said it was so we wouldn't get bored and if we ended up needing help in our classes, there was always an older student there to help. All of the kids fifteen and older, were taught in a different building out on the facility property.

The classrooms were on the first floor and they were behind each common area room. One side was for the girls and the other side was for the boys. Each room had a number on the door that would be associated with the number on the schedule that was given to each student. The time in which each child was scheduled to have each specific class, determined their learning level for that subject.

Classes started at eight thirty, then lunch at one. The facility was focused on eight major subjects; English, reading, writing, math, geography, science, history and a foreign language. The last class of the day was an extracurricular activity that each student was able to choose from on a list. Each activity was physical in order for each of us to get in our daily exercise. The list included a running club, dance class, gymnastics and a full list of sports. I chose the dance class because that was the one Rachel and Prudence chose.

Rachel had become my best friend at the facility and we did everything together. All the girls in my room would go for a run each morning before breakfast and Rachel convinced me to go with them. All of us in the room were like a little family. We all followed Prudence's rules and took guidance from Shirley, as if she was our big sister.

When Christmas came around, Susan Riley asked each of us to think of what we wanted to do when we were grown up. Once we figured it out, we were to write a list of three items that we could use for that job. She said that one of those items would be gifted to us as our Christmas present.

"What are you putting on your Christmas list?" Rachel asked me, as we sat on the floor between our beds, with a blanket draped over our heads.

"I'm going to put a big notebook, a small notebook and a fancy pen. I want to be a writer," I told her. "What about you?"

"I want to be a nurse, so I'm going to ask for a first aid kit, a testiscope and a baby doll," she told me.

"What is a testiscope?" I wondered.

"It's the thing you put in your ears and listen to the heart beat," Rachel explained.

"Oh yeah. The doctor used one of those on me when I was in the hospital," I told her.

"You know it's called a stethoscope, right?" Prudence said, peeking her head into our hiding spot.

"That's what she said, testiscope," I told her.

"Okay girls, finish up with your lists. I need to take them to Mrs. Riley," Prudence announced to everyone in the room.

After the holidays, classes resumed as normal. As my seventh birthday approached, I became more and more excited. I had seen some of the birthday parties for the other kids at the facility and Mrs. Riley and Miss Gertie always made the birthday kid feel special for the entire week of their birthday.

During the entire eight months I spent at the facility, I had recovered from my physical and emotional wounds and was having a lot of fun. Officer Leigh came to see me once a week and we talked about how I was coping with life without my mother and Auntie May.

"I like it here," I told Officer Leigh.

"Mrs. Janet Russell has found you a new home," Leigh told me.

"I don't want to leave, I want to stay here," I requested.

"I'm sorry sweetie, but this was only temporary. The department of social services is the only one who has a say of where you go."

"When do I have to go?"

"A couple of days after your birthday."

"That's next week. This is no fair," I whined.

"You get to spend your seventh birthday here, then you will start a new adventure in life," Leigh said, as if that would make me feel better.

"I guess," I said.

For my last week at the facility, the seven girls in my room, along with Miss Gertie, created a celebration for every day just for me. Each celebration lead up to my birthday.

Miss Gertie worked it out with Susan Riley that all the girls in my room and I got out of classes for the week of my birthday, so we could go on field trips everyday. Monday was the zoo, Tuesday was the aquarium, Wednesday we all went to see a movie, Thursday we went skating and Friday we went bowling.

For the weekend, Mrs. Riley had rented several bouncy castles and had them delivered to the facility so all the kids could have fun. There was a special cake for me, a piñata and several games for us to play. It was the best week of my life.

When the day came for me to leave, Susan Riley and Miss Gertie both gave me a gift that they give to each child who leaves.

The gift I received from Susan Riley was a letter telling me how I had grown since I had arrived at the facility along with a pin with the facility name on it. The gift from Miss Gertie was a pink shirt with the words, 'I survived my time at a foster care facility'.

"We are going to miss you Mackenzie," Susan Riley told me, as she hugged me. "You have really grown a lot since you have been here and I hope you continue to grow."

"Take care of yourself. Keep your strong sense of self and don't let anyone take advantage of you. You have really developed your own personality and you are a great person," Miss Gertie told me, embracing me in a hug, with tears rolling down her cheeks.

"Watch out for the damaged kids wherever you go," Joyce said, rolling her eyes at me.

Joyce and I never saw eye to eye the whole time I was at the facility, but she didn't really get along with anyone. She was a bitter young lady who had a rough life in the short time that she had been alive. There were speculations as to what had happened to her, but only Mrs. Riley and Miss Gertie really knew why she was there.

"We are going to miss you Mackenzie," Eliza said, patting my shoulder. "Of course, we won't miss the crazy blanket fort you and Rachel put up between your beds," she laughed.

When Eliza was two, her parents decided they were going on a cruise for their anniversary. She was left with a babysitter who was a college student on break. The babysitter knew it was a seven day cruise and it would take Eliza's parents another couple of days after the cruise before they would make it home.

The babysitter figured it would be about ten days and she was okay with that. After a full month and Eliza's parents still hadn't returned, the babysitter drove her to the facility and dropped her off. Eliza still hopes one day that her parents will show up to get her.

Diane and Jane had been adopted out shortly after the beginning of the new year and their beds had been empty for the past four months. Rachel was my best friend at the facility and I told her everything.

"I didn't know if this day was ever going to come and I wasn't prepared to say good bye. You are the first person I was able to open up to. I'm really going to miss you," Rachel said, as she wrapped her arms around me and cried.

I just held onto her and cried with her. Rachel lived with her parents up until she was four. Her parents emigrated to the United States just before she was born. Her parents were trying to get away from their war torn country. They wanted a safe place to raise their children.

When she was four, her parents put her to bed, then went out to the living room to watch a little television before they went to bed. As they were heading to their room, someone kicked in their front door and murdered her parents. She hid under her bed just in case the killer came for her.

She was in the house with her dead parents for a couple of days before a neighbor noticed that they hadn't seen her parents in a while. The neighbor came over and saw the door open and could hear Rachel crying.

After that, Rachel was sent to the facility and had been there ever since. She felt safe in the group facility because there were a ton of people around. Any time they talked to her about a family wanting to adopt her, she would have a panic attack as if she was reliving the moment she found her parents dead in the living room and she was alone for two days.

Rachel was one of the youngest permanent residence at the foster care facility and they didn't know if
she was ever going to leave. She only felt comfortable
around a group of people and any time she went to her
therapy sessions, Prudence, Shirley, Miss Gertie and
Mrs. Riley had to be in the room with her and her therapist in order to keep her calm.

"Don't worry kid, we will take good care of Rachel.
The card that Mrs. Riley gave you has the address to the
facility on it. Write to us when you get to your new
home and you can tell us all about it. We will write
back and Rachel and you can keep in touch. Maybe one
day y'all will meet again," Prudence told me, as Rachel
and I held onto each other and cried.

Prudence doesn't remember how old she was when
she was placed in the foster care system, but she had
been to several group homes since being placed. The
first few homes she was placed in, were temporary
housing where she would be physically and emotionally
abused. Due to the abuse, when she would have a family interested in adopting her, they would call her social
worker to pick her up after a few months, before the
adoption was finalized. They would only inform her
social worker that she was not a fit for their families.

Prudence didn't tell anyone what she did in order to
get kicked out of her potential adoptive homes, but it
was enough for her to end up at the foster care facility
until she aged out of the system.

"Don't hog her. We still have to tell her good bye to
Rachel," Shirley said, tapping Rachel on her shoulder.

"Fine," Rachel said, pulling away from me and wiping my face with her hands.

"Don't worry kid, you'll be fine. Just don't take shit from anyone," Prudence whispered in my ear, as she hugged me.

"We're going to miss you around here. I never understood your sign language, I knew it meant you didn't want to talk," Shirley told me, when it was her turn.

Shirley was a great big sister. Sometimes she had a sassy attitude with Prudence when she was told what to do, but she was generally helpful. She would only talk to Miss Gertie about anything personal, so I wasn't sure why she was there.

Officer Leigh stood in front of the doors, holding my packed bag, waiting for me to finish my farewells. The other children that lived at the facility, to which I had come into contact with, but never really communicated with, just waved as I turned to leave with Officer Leigh. It was just another group of kids I would never see again.

Sixteen

I was glad Officer Leigh had come to pick me up and escort me to my third foster home instead of Janet Russell. I learned so much at the facility and how to take care of myself and I wanted to tell Leigh about it.

"I know this is hard on you, but eventually you will find a permanent home. If you have a family interested in adopting you, take hold of the opportunity and embrace the family life. I promise you will have a family again, one day," Officer Leigh said, as she drove down the long winding private road away from the foster care facility.

"It's okay. I talked to the girls in the room and I learned a lot about being in the foster care system," I told her.

"Oh yeah? What did you learn?"

"Well, Prudence, my room mother, she taught me to never take shit from anyone. She told me that I was too sweet to be in the foster care system and that I was going to need to toughen up and use the attitude I had with Betty Warren to my advantage. She told me that some group homes can be rough and I need to protect myself from not only the foster parents, but also from some of the other kids."

"Sounds like Prudence has had a rough time adjusting to the foster care system. I don't know if that is the best advise. I think that you being a sweet kid is what is going to help you get adopted."

"But Prudence told me how some of the kids in the foster care system can end up on the streets, or in jail," I explained.

"There are also those who go on to do great things. I think you are going to be one of the great ones," she told me.

"Family is overrated. If my own mother could just dump me, why would I want another one, but I will need to know how to survive the years I will possibly bounce around from foster home to foster home before I stop at a permanent home. I didn't feel like I had enough time to learn survival at the facility, but Prudence assured me I was ready. Tell me about my new home and the foster parents."

Leigh glanced at me as she began to tell me about where I would soon be living. "Glen and Ramona Cavos are busy executives who haven't had time to have their own children, so they temporarily house one foster child at a time. You could be spending a lot of time with their live in nanny that they keep on hand for their foster children."

"So that means I won't be spending any real time with them. That's cool. I have been spending a lot of time with other kids anyway," I told her, as she pulled up to a house.

The home seemed simple from the outside. Officer Leigh rang the doorbell and a woman who introduced herself as Mary opened the door.

"Hello Mary. This is Mackenzie. She is the new foster child that will be living here," Leigh told her.

"Please come in. Mrs. Ramona and Mr. Glen are working right now. Mackenzie will be able to meet them at dinner," Mary informed.

"Am I able to speak with them right now?" Leigh asked.

"I'm sorry, but they don't allow distractions when they are working. I will be showing Mackenzie to her room and get her settled in," Mary told her, taking my bag from Leigh.

"Okay sweetie. Please be good. Both Janet Russell and I will be checking on you regularly to make sure you are doing okay," Leigh told me, as she hugged me to leave.

Once Leigh had left, Mary took me to the room I would be staying in. The house was filled with extravagant items. It seemed as though they spent their money on materialistic items for the inside of their home, rather than purchasing a mansion.

I stayed with Ramona and Glen Cavos up to my eighth birthday. I barely ever saw them and Mary was just for show when Officer Leigh and Janet Russell visited. They were a busy couple, who basically wanted a foster child in their home in order to feel as though they were contributing to charity.

Officer Leigh and Janet Russell stopped by separately about once a month to check on me. Ramona and Glen Cavos would never allow me to be alone in the room with them during the visits. The couple would talk about how proud they were of themselves to be able to help a child in need.

On my eighth birthday, when Officer Leigh came to visit and give me my birthday present, the couple left us alone. I finally had my chance to tell her how I felt about living there.

"I don't like it here. They don't like me being here. Tell Mrs. Russell she needs to find me a new home," I told Officer Leigh.

"They seem very happy to have you here," Leigh said.

"They like the idea of having an orphan in their home. They tell people I'm a charity. They appreciate the paycheck they receive."

"Mackenzie, you don't know that."

"Every time the check comes in, they talk about what they can buy for themselves to make them look good. I am used as their servant when they have dinner parties for their friends. I only get to eat what is left over after they eat, or what is left over after a party."

"What happened with Mary?"

"She is their assistant. Mary was mostly doing things for them. I have barely ever seen them and every so often I would see Mary. Twice Mr. Cavos walked past me in the living room and I couldn't remember who he was."

"Have you had any family time with Glen and Ramona?"

"No, and I feel that I am old enough now to be able to navigate if I were to leave. Tell Mrs. Russell I will only be here for another week before I take this matter into my own hands," I explained.

"Please don't do that. I will call her as soon as I leave here and see what she can do for you," Leigh told me.

"How are you doing in here?" Ramona asked, as she entered the room.

"We're fine," I responded, rolling my eyes.

"Can I get either of you something?" Ramona said.

"No ma'am, thank you," Officer Leigh told her.

"Mackenzie, I have just ordered a cake to be delivered for your birthday and it should be here soon. Officer, would you like to stay for cake?" Ramona said, coming over to sit on the sofa next to me.

"No thank you. I need to get back to my patrol. Janet Russell should be here tomorrow to check on Mackenzie," Leigh told Ramona before turning to me. "Happy birthday sweet girl. I'll let you know what I find out."

I hugged her before she left. Ramona waved through the open doorway before closing and dead bolting the door. She turned and looked down at me, pursing her lips.

"What did you tell her?" Ramona asked, stepping closer to me.

"Nothing. We just talked about my birthday and she said I have grown up a lot since we met," I told her, backing away.

"You better keep your mouth shut. If you mess with my paycheck, you will be sorry. Go to your room until I call you to serve us for dinner."

"I thought you said you ordered me cake for my birthday."

"Please, I would never spend my money on you. I was glad the cop decided to leave because I didn't have an excuse as to why the cake hadn't shown up. I don't care about your birthday. It doesn't effect me in any way," Ramona said, before turning and walking away.

I went into the room I had been staying in and started packing my bag. I knew that when Officer Leigh said Janet Russell would be visiting me the next day, that meant I would be leaving. Even if she wasn't there to pick me up, I would cause a scene that would set off Mr. and Mrs. Cavos, so Janet would take me out of the home any way.

Luckily for me, when Janet Russell showed up the next day, she informed them that she was able to find me more permanent housing and I would be going with her. I ran to the room and snatched up my fully packed bag and ran straight to the front door to wait for her to talk to the couple.

"Please don't take our little girl. We have enjoyed having her here this past year," Ramona told Janet.

"We can find you another foster child to stay with you," Janet informed.

"How long do you think that will take? The last time it was almost three months before we got Mackenzie," Glen asked.

"Contact my office tomorrow and I will let you know if there is a child who needs a home. Thank you for allowing Mackenzie to stay with you," Janet said, as she ushered me out of the house.

"Finally. I don't know how much longer I would be able to live in there," I told Janet, as we walked out to her car.

"What happened in that house?" Janet asked, once we were on the road headed toward my next home.

"Have you spoken to Officer Leigh?" I asked her.

"I did. She told me what you said yesterday."

"Oh good. That means you are up to speed with the situation."

Seventeen

"Can you please change your attitude about this? I understand you didn't choose your situation, but you could at least try fitting in with the family?" Janet requested.

"Fine, so where are you taking me today?" I asked, rolling my eyes.

"You are going to the home of Carolyn and Mitchell Donovan. They tend to only foster young children under the age of six. They feel like the younger children are easier to teach and mould into functioning members of society. When I informed them about your rough life so far, they decided to take you in."

"Have you investigated them to make sure I would be safe?" I wanted to know.

"I did look into their foster care background. There haven't been any complaints about this couple and they seem to be chosen to take care of foster children regularly," Janet explained.

"Of course there haven't been any complaints. The only children they have in their house can't exactly communicate their feelings properly," I told her.

"Alright, that's enough. Please be respectful to Mr. and Mrs. Donovan," Janet said.

"When we get there, I will find out how much respect they deserve," I stated, staring out the window.

When we arrived at the Donovan home, I knew it was going to be a challenge. First, the mobile home looked as though it hadn't been taken care of since it had been manufactured decades before. Second, the yard was overgrown and there was a path of fabricated slate leading up to their front steps through the yard.

I couldn't help but wonder if I was going to be used to take care of things around the house, seeing as I would be the oldest child in the home. I didn't let on to Janet that I felt as though this was not going to be a place that I would stay for long.

As we walked up the pathway toward the porch, the front door opened and a heavy woman with disheveled dark hair emerged holding a baby of about six months. She had a lit cigarette hanging out of her mouth and five more children gathered around her.

"You must be Mackenzie. I'm Carolyn and my husband Mitch should be home from work soon. Come on in and I will show you the room you will be stayin' in," the woman said, with a thick southern accent.

Janet and I stepped inside and immediately the smell of cigarette smoke and urine hit me hard. All of the children looked as though they hadn't been bathed in months and their clothes were dirty. I looked up at Janet, silently pleading with her not to leave me there.

"Try to fit in here. I don't know how many more homes I can find for you to live in until someone decides to adopt you," Janet leaned down and whispered in my ear.

"Are you going to be living here with us?" one of the dirty children asked.

"Now Joshie, don't bother 'er just yet. We'll all sit down and talk to 'er once the lady leaves," Carolyn told the child.

"Okay, well I guess I will leave you to get acquainted. Mackenzie, Leigh will be stopping by at the end of the week to see how you are getting along. Please don't cause any trouble, or tell her any lies," Janet told me, before she left.

"Okay, well you're gonna be stayin' in the room with the baby and the two young-ins. This one here is Brittney. She's a little hard to handle at night, but you'll do fine. Brittney is six months old and still won't sleep through the night," Carolyn told me, passing the baby to me.

She smelled as though she needed a diaper change several hours ago and a bath. Her clothes were dingy and she was drooling more than I thought a baby should, but I wasn't sure.

"Startin' from the oldest, you got Joshie. He's six. Then ere's Ashley. She's five. Then Nickie. He's four. He don't talk much, but when he's got somein' to say, he just won't shut up. Next is Heather. She's three. And last is Davie. He's two. If he grunts when he's askin' fer somein' you make him say it. We need to learn how to use our words round here," Carolyn introduced the children to me, then walked over to the sofa, grabbed another cigarette out of the pack sitting on the table and lit it with the butt end of the one that had been in her mouth.

I stood there holding the baby and looking down at the five other children. They had circled around me and seemed to be waiting for me to tell them what to do.

"Y'all want to show me the room I'm going to be sleeping in?" I said to the kids.

Joshie grabbed my bag and dragged it down the hallway to the first bedroom on the right. The next door down the hall was the bathroom and the room at the end of the hall belonged to the three oldest children.

All seven of us entered the room and I looked around. There was a crib and a dirty king sized mattress in the room. There weren't any sheets on the mattress, but there were several blankets and pillows. The mattress at the bottom of the crib was stained with urine and feces and a blanket was balled up in one corner.

I retrieved a diaper from a box under the crib and a package of wipes. I had never changed a diaper before, but I was going to teach myself in order to take care of these kids. Luckily, Brittney was the only one in diapers, so I didn't have to worry about the toddlers.

I laid Brittney down on the mattress and removed the dirty clothes she was wearing. I looked at the soggy diaper and decided that the only way I could learn was to just do it. I removed the dirty diaper and pulled out a wipe and started to clean her up. Every part of her body that was covered by the diaper was red and irritated. She cried as I did my best to clean off the dried feces from her bottom.

"Shut that baby up. I'm tryin' to watch my stories," Carolyn yelled, from the living room.

Once I had cleaned her up, I replaced her diaper with a clean one, then picked her up and embraced her in my arms apologizing to her. Once she had calmed down, I set her back on the mattress where the other children sat.

When Mitchell Donovan arrived home that first evening, he informed me that I was to feed the children and get them to bed, then I was to make them dinner. Once the two of them were done eating, then and only then was I allowed to make myself something to eat.

'Wonderful,' I thought. *'I'm back to taking care of myself and serving others, except this time I have to take care of someone else's children.'*

I was in charge of taking care of the children for the year that I lived in the Donovan home. I was worried about getting all of the children out of the deplorable conditions in the house, but I knew Janet didn't care about the conditions we were living in, so I just left it alone. That way I would know the children were being taken care of. Considering the fact that I cleaned the house and the children, they started calling me mommy.

Every time Leigh came to visit, I was only allowed to visit with her outside. Carolyn would tell me to take the kids out to play and not to come back inside until Officer Leigh was gone.

When Christmas came around, I understood why there weren't any toys in the house. There weren't any presents for any of us. The Donovans didn't even decorate for the holidays. Every day was the same no matter what the date was.

The young kids revolved through the house as they were removed for adoption. By the time I left, the kids that were there were not the same kids I had been introduced to when I had first arrived.

Carolyn chain smoked in the house and mostly just watched television. I had finally had enough when they agreed to take on a physically handicapped six year old that was unable to communicate and would need around the clock care. She was in a wheel chair and had the mind of a toddler. She would need to be fed, bathed and have her diaper changed. By that time I was nine years old and did not want to change the diaper of a child that was large enough to injure me.

I finally revealed to Officer Leigh as to the conditions of the house and what was going on. The day that the disabled child was supposed to be dropped off, Leigh showed up with Janet and a social services van. We were all going to be removed from the home.

Janet Russell took the other children in the van and Leigh drove me to my fifth foster home.

Eighteen

"So, where am I going now?" I asked Leigh.

"The new home you are going to has two loving foster parents. Candice and Walter Holmes. They have been fostering children for the past ten years and live in a great neighborhood that is zoned to a top rated school district. They only foster two children at a time so they have time to spend with each child. I will expect you to be on your best behavior," Leigh lectured

"I can only promise that I will treat them with the same respect they show me. If I am going to be treated like a slave again, you can guarantee that my disrespectful side is willing to show. I don't want to be taken advantage of anymore," I told her.

"I know that Mr. and Mrs. Holmes genuinely enjoy taking care of the foster kids they are in charge of. The payment they receive for each child goes into a savings account for that child. They continue putting money into it, even after that child has left their home. It's to help the child when they are old enough to be out on their own. Sort of like starter money," she told me.

"So in other words, they are trying to prepare the children for grown-up life. Well, I tell you one thing, I won't take shit from any other kid, but I definitely won't take anymore shit from grown-ups."

"Whoa, where did that language come from?"

"My mother use to say bad words. I already knew them, but now my life has become a steaming pile of shit."

"What happened to that sweet little girl I saved a few years ago?"

"She's gone. I'm the new Mackenzie. Here to survive until I am old enough to live on my own."

"You're nine. Where is all of this coming from?"

"I've lived with older kids at Betty Warren's house and when I was at the facility. Miss Gertie helped me work through some emotions. I took care of myself when I stayed with Glen and Ramona Cavos. I took care of other small children at the Donovan house. Trust me, I have changed."

"You've grown up a lot from that scared little girl I first met."

"I'm still that scared little girl. I've just learned how to hide my fear and only look after myself. I'm not a grown-up, yet," I told her.

"I didn't say you were a grown-up, I said you have grown up. I just mean you are maturing and becoming a lovely, but profane young lady," She told me.

"Other than the facility, the foster homes I have been sent to live at have sucked. I hope this one is better. What can you tell me about the other child in the Holmes house?" I was nervous, but held my head high, determined not to show it.

"What makes you think there is already another child there?" Leigh asked.

"You said they foster two children at a time. That means they had two, one left and I'm the replacement.

So, tell me about the other kid," I responded indignantly.

"Okay, little miss smarty pants. His name is Johnny Taylor. He is ten years old. His mother died during his birth. He was a very cranky baby and because they were unable to calm him, they decided to keep him in the hospital to keep an eye on him. He spent the first few months of his life in the hospital under constant supervision. He was eventually released into the foster care system, but he would never stay at one house for too long," Leigh explained.

"Is he okay now?" I wondered.

"Every so often he has fits of rage, but Mr. and Mrs. Holmes are working with him on that."

"I'm not going to be in any danger, am I?"

"No sweetheart. They have figured out how to handle him and how to keep the other child safe."

"As long as you are sure that I am safe. Can I make a request though?"

"Sure, what is it?"

"If I don't like it there, can I go back to the foster care facility? I always got along with the kids at the facility and I miss spending time with Rachel."

"You have to understand, the facility runs on private donations and adoption fees. It costs money for each child to live there. The children are generally housed at the facility for a short time. It's basically a home for kids who are new to the foster care system, or were abused in a foster home. If you were fifteen or older, it would be different. You would only be there for three years before you would age out of the foster care system. After that, they require you to get a job and assist you with paying your own bills, including renting a room, they don't just throw you out. They do, however, insist that you be well behaved and at this time, you are no longer a candidate to live at the facility."

"Shirley was only thirteen when I was there and she said she is learning how to be a teacher at the facility, so she doesn't have to leave. When she first got there, she was only twelve, so she will be there longer than three years," I told her, with a sassy tone.

"That is a special training program they offer and it is only available for five children under the age of fifteen, but you have to be older than ten. How about when you turn fifteen, if you are still unhappy, I will see what I can do for you, but you will have to change your attitude," she told me.

"That's a long time, but I'm going to hold you to that," I responded, as Officer Leigh pulled up to a large two story home.

"This is it," Leigh said, shifting the car into park.

"This house is huge. Are you sure there is only one other kid living here and not nine?" I said, overwhelmed by the size of the house.

The grey bricked home had a dirt brown front door and two white, single garage doors. The two story home was shaped like an L. There was a window that looked into the garage. I opened the back door to the car and got out to look into the window. I saw two bikes, a box of toys and a minivan, through the window.

"Well, let's go inside and see how big it really is," Leigh said after she retrieved my bag from the trunk of her car.

I walked through the grass over to the driveway, where Leigh was waiting for me and stared at the front of the house.

"I bet it's going to be big inside too," I told her.

"Well, come on Mackenzie. Let's go up to the front door so we can meet the people you are going to be living with."

Leigh grabbed my hand and led me to the door. She reached up and pressed the button for the doorbell and we waited.

When the door opened, a slim brunette in her mid-forties was standing on the other side. She was wearing jeans and an oversized sweatshirt with one side hanging off her left shoulder.

"Well, hello there. You must be Mackenzie. I'm Candice Holmes and this is my husband, Walter. We have been looking forward to meeting you," Mrs. Holmes said, just as a man stepped up behind her from inside the house.

"Why don't you two come inside, so we can get to know Mackenzie a little better," Mr. Holmes said, placing his hands on his wife's shoulders and gently pulling her away from the open doorway, so Leigh and I could step inside.

Walter Holmes had short, thinning hair. He wore black slacks and a white button down dress shirt with the top two buttons unbuttoned.

Leigh placed her hand on my back, between my shoulder blades and ushered me over the threshold. We stepped into the foyer and Mrs. Holmes closed the door.

Ten feet inside the door was the stairs to the second floor. To the right was a den area with a desk and book shelves. To the left was the living room. Behind the living room was the kitchen and behind the stairs was the dining room.

"Let's go over into the living room. I'll get Johnny from his room and Candice can get refreshments," Walter said, motioning toward the sofa in the living room as his wife walked through the archway between the living room and the kitchen.

Leigh and I wandered over and sat down on their tan sofa as Mr. Holmes headed up the stairs. As soon as he was out of ear shot, I tapped Leigh on her knee.

"They lock the kids in their rooms?" I told her.

"You don't know that. Maybe he's just reading a book, or likes being alone. When he comes down you can ask him," Leigh said.

"Well, now that we are inside, this house is still huge," I told Leigh.

"Yes, it is," Leigh said, looking around the room.

The tan sofa was paired with a matching love seat and recliner. There wasn't a television in the room, but I was use to not watching T.V., so it didn't really bother me. There was a large photo of the couple over the fireplace.

The walls had framed photos of children. Some were group photos of the couple with two children and some were single photos of just one child. In the group photos, the couple was always with one boy and one girl. Just as I wondered if one of the photos was of the boy currently in the house, Mr. Holmes appeared with Johnny.

"Johnny, this is Mackenzie. She's going to be staying with us for a while. Say hi, Johnny," Mr. Holmes said, as Mrs. Holmes appeared with a tray of cookies, tea cups and a tea kettle.

"Hi, Johnny," the boy said.

"Cute. Say hello to Mackenzie, please," Mrs. Holmes told him, setting the tray down on the coffee table.

"Hello to Mackenzie. My name is Johnny. I'm ten years old and I'm a smart ass," Johnny said, picking up a cookie.

"Johnny, language," Mr. Holmes said, as I giggled.

"We are still working on what he says, how he says it and when he says it. I'm sorry he spoke that way in front of you, Mackenzie," Mrs. Holmes said, pouring tea into the tea cups.

"That's okay. I've learned not to take shit from anyone," I said.

Johnny laughed as Mrs. Holmes choked on her sip of tea and coughed into her cup. Leigh grabbed my arm and gave me a disappointed mom look.

"Mackenzie, these nice people are welcoming you into their home. You need to obey their rules. They don't allow that kind of language in their house. Please respect their rules," Leigh chastised.

"Sorry ma'am. Mrs. Holmes, Mr. Holmes, I appreciate your hospitality," I said, respectfully.

"Thank you, Mackenzie," Mrs. Holmes said, as she dabbed her mouth with a napkin.

"So, would you like a tour of the house?" Mr. Holmes asked.

"Absolutely sir," I responded.

"Johnny, why don't you show Mackenzie where to put her things and show her around while the grown-ups talk," Mr. Holmes said.

"Sure, come on Mackenzie and I'll show you to your room, madam," Johnny said, bowing and motioning toward the stairs.

I looked at Leigh and she nodded. I picked up my bag and followed Johnny upstairs. At the top of the stairs was a large open room set up with four reclining chairs with cup holders in the right arm of each chair. The chairs all faced a very large T.V.

"That's the movie room. Every Friday and Saturday night is movie night. Mr. and Mrs. Holmes order pizza on Friday and Chinese food on Saturday and we watch a movie after dinner those nights," Johnny informed me. "The door to the right is always closed. That is Mr. and Mrs. Holmes' room. This first room on the left is mine and the room next to it, is yours. We each have our own bathroom and privacy whenever we want it. Go ahead and put your bag in there and I'll take you downstairs and show you the homework room."

I turned and opened the door to the room I was going to be staying in. The room was huge and had framed photos of several girls on the walls. I assumed they were the girls that had stayed in that room before me. The walls were white, the furniture was white and the sheets on the bed were black. I placed my bag on the floor in front of the dresser and rejoined Johnny out in the hallway.

"They keep the decorations to a minimum so you can decorate your room how ever you want. The only thing you can't change is the walls," Johnny told me.

"Is it nice living here?" I asked him. "Why were you locked in your room when Officer Leigh and I got here?"

"I wasn't locked in my room. When they told me there was a new girl coming to live with us, I asked if she was going to be a little bitch like the last one. The last girl who was here before you used to cry every time I had a fit of rage. She was only here for a couple of months before she cried to her social worker that she was scared of me and wanted to leave. Mr. and Mrs. Holmes don't like it when I use certain language, so I was told to go into my room and calm down," Johnny explained.

"But they didn't lock you in?"

"No, I wasn't locked in. Mr. Holmes created a meditation session for me when I get angry and being in my room alone helps me focus. I don't mind. I get to think of ways to escape in case I get moved to another house."

"You like living here?"

"The foster parents are nice, helpful and really seem to care. They don't adopt, they only foster and once they feel that you are ready for adoption, they inform your social worker and you move to a new home with people who want to adopt you. They like taking broken foster kids and get them to trust again. You must have had a rough life to end up here," Johnny said.

"My mother abandoned me when I was six, the first foster home I went to, the foster mother beat me and I was in the hospital for a couple of days. I spent about a year at a boarding school foster care facility, a year with a couple of people who just liked the fact that having a foster child meant they were receiving a paycheck just to house a homeless child, and for the past year, I was living in a house with a couple of disgusting human beings who forced me to take care of the other foster kids. Those kids were between the ages of six months old, to four years old. I hate moving around and I hope I get to stay here for a while," I said.

"It depends on my rage and how you handle it," Johnny told me, walking over to one of the movie chairs.

"How bad is it?" I asked, sitting in the chair next to him.

"Sometimes I become violent and don't know how to control it. Mrs. Holmes takes the girl foster out during my rage spells and they do girly things. Mr. Holmes speaks calmly to me and depending on what triggered my rage, he tries to tell me how it doesn't matter and how life is better now. I see a therapist twice a week to try to understand my rage, but sometimes I can't control it."

"Have you ever hurt anyone?"

"Only once. When I was four, I was at a foster home for kids who were born addicted to drugs. There were about fifteen of us there and I was the youngest. I had seen an older boy slash another kid with a knife on the arm. It was so deep and there was so much blood, the kid who got cut ended up with twenty five stitches in his arm and the kid who cut him. Well, his social worker took him to a new home and that was the last time I saw him.

"I hated the fact that the foster parents ignored us and we basically took care of ourselves. I wanted to go to a new home too, so I took a knife and slashed up one of the other kids. I stabbed him in his stomach and had to be pulled off of him. I was covered in his blood. My social worker took me to an institution where they medicated me for a year. When they decided I was okay to go to a new foster home, I came here and have been here ever since."

"What happened to the kid you stabbed?"

"I don't know. No one ever told me."

"So you have been here since you were five?" I asked.

"Yep, and as long as they continue helping me through my rage spells, I will stay here as long as they will let me," Johnny said.

"If Mr. and Mrs. Holmes don't adopt, how are you able to stay here as long as you want?"

"It's not that I'm staying here because I want to, even though I do, it's more that no other foster family, or prospective adoptive family, wants a child with anger issues."

"Kenzie, I'm going to leave now," Leigh said, from the bottom of the stairs.

I stood up and rushed down the stairs. I jumped over the last step and landed in front of Leigh. I wrapped my arms around her waist and gave her a tight squeeze.

"I'll stop by at least once a week to check in on you for a while," Leigh told me.

"Okay, I talked to Johnny. I think I might like it here," I told her, as I pulled away from her.

"I think you might like it too," Leigh said, stroking my hair.

Mr. Holmes opened the front door and walked Leigh to her car. Johnny came down the stairs and stood on the bottom step.

"Okay kids, it's Friday night, pizza night. Mackenzie, what's your favorite pizza?" Mrs. Holmes asked.

"I don't know," I said.

"Haven't you ever had pizza before?" Johnny asked, puzzled.

"No, before my mother abandoned me, I ate home cooked meals at the neighbor's house. The few places I stayed at before I came here, I had to find food in the house to eat. I had stayed at a foster home facility and their food was scheduled. Pancakes for breakfast, soup and sandwiches for lunch and each night's dinner was themed. Pasta with salad Monday, tacos with rice Tuesday, asian Wednesday, grilled chicken and veggies Thursday, fresh fish and French fries Friday, healthy Saturday and left over Sunday. I've never had pizza," I told them.

"You've never had pizza? That's okay. We usually order one cheese and one pepperoni. How about we add a supreme to the mix and you can try one of each and see which one you like the best," Mr. Holmes said, as he came back into the house and closed the door.

"Sounds good," I said, as Mr. Holmes headed to the kitchen to order the pizza, then turned to Candice, "Mrs. Holmes, can I ask you a question?"

"Absolutely sweetie. What is it?"

"Do you like to run?"

"I do. I run every morning, three miles. Why do you ask?" she wondered.

"When I was staying at the facility, I started running with some of the other girls every morning before breakfast and I would like to start doing it again. I don't want to go by myself and was wondering if I could go with you," I told her.

"It would be wonderful to have a morning running buddy," she said, smiling from ear to ear.

"Great, I am awake at six every morning, so I will be ready to go whenever you are in the morning," I told her.

"Man, six in the morning is early as hell," Johnny said.

"Johnny, language," Mrs. Holmes said.

"I know, sorry, but that just seems really early," he said.

"It is, but the earlier you get your workout done, the more time you have for other things throughout the rest of the day," I told him.

"Well, while Walter is ordering pizza, how about you two go upstairs and pick out a movie for after dinner," Mrs. Holmes suggested.

Johnny and I raced upstairs and he showed me their extensive video collection. He opened the doors on a large cabinet in the corner of the T.V. room. I walked over and began perusing the movies as if I knew what I was looking for.

"So, what do you want to watch?" Johnny asked me, bouncing on his toes next to me.

"Can I be honest?" I wondered.

"Of course you can."

"I have only seen one movie in my life and it was the night I stayed with Officer Leigh."

"When did you stay with Officer Leigh and what movie did you watch?"

"The night my mother abandoned me, Officer Leigh rescued me and I spent my first night as an orphan at Officer Leigh's house. We watched *The Little Mermaid*."

"Okay, well there are two things wrong with that. One, it's a girl movie and two, it's for babies. Being in the foster care system will force you to grow up fast. How about I pick the movie and you just go with it?" Johnny suggested.

"That's easier for me. Whatever you pick, I'm sure it will be great," I told him.

"Awesome, because I really like the movie *Ghostbusters*. The guys in this movie are so funny."

He chose the video, closed the cabinet and placed the movie on top of the T.V. for us to watch after we ate. Johnny and I ran down the stairs and joined our foster parents in the kitchen.

"Are you. allergic to anything Mackenzie?" Mr. Holmes asked, as he pulled the phone away from his ear and rested it on his shoulder.

"I don't think so, but I guess we will find out when I eat the pizza," I said, laughing.

"Well, okay then. Put it all on there," Mr. Holmes said, to the person on the other end of the phone.

"Did you two pick out a movie?" Mrs. Holmes asked, after her husband hung up the phone.

"Sure did. *Ghostbusters*," I told them.

"Johnny, you should have let Mackenzie pick out the movie," Mr. Holmes said.

"I told him to pick out the movie. I haven't actually watched T.V., so it is perfect. He can watch a movie he likes and I get to experience a whole new world," I explained.

"I guess it worked out then," Mr. Holmes said.

"Great, this is going to be a great night," Mrs. Holmes said.

"I think I'm going to like it here. Y'all are nice," I said, smiling.

"And we are going to like having you here," Mr. Holmes said, patting me on my head.

Nineteen

Living with Johnny Taylor and Candice and Walter Holmes was a blessing. When Thanksgiving rolled around, Mrs. Holmes asked if I wanted to help make dinner.

"Really? You want me to help?" I said, beaming.

"Absolutely. It would be like a mother/daughter bonding moment," Candice said, playing with my hair.

"That would be amazing. Thank you so much."

"Also, would you like to invite Officer Leigh to come over for the day as well?"

"That would be like having my whole family together at one time."

"We can go shopping this afternoon and pick up everything we need for Thursday. I have a list, but go ahead and call Officer Leigh and find out if there is anything specific she likes for Thanksgiving."

"Awesome. This is going to be the best holiday ever," I said, as I grabbed the phone.

For Christmas, Johnny helped Mr. Holmes put up the lights on the outside of the house and I helped Mrs. Holmes put up the tree and decorate with the ornaments. Mrs. Holmes had also purchased a special ornament for me as my first Christmas with them. Johnny already had one and he was able to put it on the tree himself.

All four of us decorated the inside of the house. There was garland and Santa's village. On the front lawn there was a large nativity scene.

On Christmas morning, the living room was over run with presents. Johnny and I ran down the stairs, practically rock star sliding on our knees across the floor.

"Hold on now. Johnny, you know we eat breakfast before we open presents," Mrs. Holmes said, as she entered the living room, wiping her hands on a kitchen towel.

"This is way more than I expected. You really didn't have to get me anything. Being a part of your family is the best gift I could ever ask for," I told Mrs. Holmes, as Johnny and I stood up and headed toward the kitchen.

"We have enjoyed having you here. You are a part of our family and this is our way to show you how much we have enjoyed having you here," Mrs. Holmes told me, as she embraced me.

After we had opened all the gifts under the tree and cleaned up the mountain of wrapping paper that had accumulated on the floor, Officer Leigh had stopped by with presents for both me and Johnny.

A week after Christmas, mom and dad Holmes took Johnny and me to see a fireworks show to ring in the new year. It was the most beautiful thing I had seen in my nine and a half years.

After the New Year, Officer Leigh was visiting me less and less all the time, but I was okay with that. I had begun referring to Candice as mom and Walter as dad. Johnny was my brother in all aspects of the word and I was happy with my new family.

I had lived with them for almost two years. In that time, Johnny only had two rage spells, which happened in the first year I was there and each time Candice would take me to go shopping and get our nails done. There were a couple of times he would start getting angry and I would calm him down. Johnny's rage wasn't as bad as they made it seem. That was until my eleventh birthday came around.

Mrs. Holmes had made me a two tiered strawberry cake with vanilla frosting and sliced strawberries on top. Johnny and I helped put the mix in the pan and placed it in the oven. She set up a smaller pan for the top tier and prepped it to go into the oven once the bottom came out.

"It's been really nice having you around these past two years. Don't you think so Johnny?" Mrs. Holmes said.

"I hope she stays with us forever," Johnny stated matter-of-factly.

"Forever and ever," I said, as Johnny and I laughed.

"I don't know if that's possible. Janet will be visiting tomorrow to check on how Mackenzie is doing and decide whether or not it is time for her to leave," Candice informed.

"She let me stay for a whole extra year when she came to visit me on my last birthday. I like it here and I don't want to go," I said.

"It's been like a real family with her here. I don't want her to go," Johnny said, his tone becoming aggressive.

He reached out and grabbed me, embracing me into a hug. I wrapped my arms around him at the same time.

"Johnny, you know it is not our decision. The social worker is the one who decides where each of you children go to live," Mr. Holmes told him, as he joined us in the kitchen.

"It's not fair. I have been here for seven years and I have seen the girls come and go. Why can't one of them just stay here with us?" Johnny said, throwing things across the room.

"Johnny, let's go upstairs to your room," Walter suggested.

"I don't need to go upstairs. I need life to go my way for once," Johnny said, throwing himself on the floor like a toddler.

"Johnny, this is not how you should act. Get off the floor," I said, standing over him.

He sat up, with his legs straight out in front of him and looked up at me. I glared down at him, waiting for him to realize that his actions were unwarranted. He took a deep breath in before releasing a loud, high pitched, angry scream.

"All right, that's it. Come on Johnny. Let's go upstairs," Walter told him, hooking his elbows under Johnny's arms and placing Johnny into a standing position.

"This isn't fair. The foster care system is total bullshit!" Johnny yelled, on his way up the stairs, turning over furniture and throwing photos off the wall on his way.

"I'll take care of him. You two finish the cake and as soon as he has calmed down, we will return to join you," Walter said, patting my hand.

"Do we need to leave?" I asked Candice, as soon as Walter went up the stairs.

"No sweetie. Walter will take care of it. I can talk to Janet when she comes tomorrow and see if you can stay here a little longer. He has been so much calmer since you have lived here. You are a perfect fit to our family," Mrs. Holmes said.

"I like it here. Maybe Janet will think this family is a perfect fit for me and she will let me stay. I know your home is only supposed to be temporary, but your house has been the best place I have ever lived," I told her, wrapping my arms around her waist.

"I know we have all enjoyed having you here this past year," Candice said, hugging me back. "Unfortunately, our house is only a stopping point for children who are having a rough life. We are here to help you with your anger and expressing your emotions the right way in order for you to have a normal life. Social services just makes sure you are happy and have accepted your destiny in the system. Before you become too comfortable here, they move you to another home. It's so we can help another child who needs us," Candice explained, as I pulled away from her.

"I thought social workers were supposed to cater to the best interest of the child? Why remove a child from a home where they are happy? I don't understand," I told her, dipping my finger into the cake batter and licking it off.

"I would rather burn this house down so none of us could stay here," Johnny yelled from upstairs.

I looked up at Mrs. Holmes to see her reaction to Johnny's outburst. Her eyes were wide, as she raised her eyebrows. We could hear the muffled sound of Walter's voice as he spoke calmly to Johnny.

"I don't care. I don't want her to leave. I could threaten her social worker to leave Mackenzie here, or she'll be sorry," Johnny shouted, trailing off by the end of his statement.

The door to Johnny's room opened and Mr. Holmes spoke. "Johnny, you know how the system works. Now, either come down stairs and enjoy what time you have with Mackenzie, or stay here in your room and sulk. The choice is yours."

It only took a few more moments before we heard Johnny and Walter's footsteps as they descended the staircase. The timer on the oven sounded and Mrs. Holmes removed the first tier of my birthday cake from the oven and replaced it with the top tier.

"Are you ready to have some fun Johnny?" I asked, handing him one of the party hats Candice had picked up from the party store. "We can watch *Howard the Duck* and eat cake."

"I guess we should enjoy the time we have left together before you get taken away," Johnny said, smiling and leaning his head on my shoulder.

"I guess I should get the spaghetti started, so once the cake is done I can put the garlic bread in the oven and everything can be done at the same time," Candice said, kissing me on the forehead.

Johnny calmed down and Candice poured the pasta into the boiling water, then pulled the second tier of the cake out of the oven, replacing it with the garlic bread. Candice assembled the pieces of the cake together and gave both Johnny and me a container of frosting and a couple of spoons.

"I think one of us should have a spoon to scoop the frosting, while the other one spreads it with a knife," Johnny suggested, picking up a butter knife.

"Maybe you should take the spoon and let me have the knife. You can be a little unpredictable," I told Johnny, laughing.

"Oh, you think you're funny now?" Johnny said, scooping his finger in the frosting and swiping a dollop on my nose.

Both Candice and Walter laughed with us. Candice took the knife, then started heating up the sauce as Johnny and I frosted the cake and Walter went upstairs to their bedroom.

"Are you going to leave that frosting on your nose?" Johnny asked, as we slathered the last of the white frosting along the side of the cake.

"Did you want to lick it off?" I said, wagging my head back and forth at him.

"Sure," Johnny laughed, grabbing my shoulders and running his tongue from the tip of my nose all the way to my forehead.

"Ewe, Johnny," I giggled, as I wiped down my nose with my hand.

"You told me to do it," Johnny said, picking up the butter knife again, scraping the inside of the frosting container, then licking the frosting off the knife.

"Johnny, don't lick the knife. You could cut yourself," Candice told him, holding out her hand.

Johnny handed her the knife and Walter reappeared in the kitchen. Candice lifted the pasta pot and poured the boiling water and noodles into the colander that was in the bottom of the sink.

"The spaghetti is almost ready. Once we are done eating, we will head up to watch the movie," Candice said, as she transferred the pasta into a large glass bowl and poured the sauce over top.

The four of us sat at the table, just as we always did and enjoyed our family dinner. After we had finished, Johnny and I helped clean up, while Walter made popcorn.

Just as we were heading toward the stairs to watch the movie, the doorbell rang. I ran to answer the door with Candice and Walter close behind. Officer Leigh stood on the other side of the door with a birthday present.

"Happy birthday Kenzie," Leigh said.

"Thank you," I exclaimed, lurching out the door and wrapping my arms around her waist, embracing her.

"Please Officer Leigh, come inside," Candice said.

"Thank you. I have something for Mackenzie for her birthday," Leigh told her, as she entered the house with me still attached to her waist.

Johnny sat down on the stairs and watched us in the living room through the gaps in the banister railing. Leigh placed the box on the coffee table. I sat down on the floor in front of the box while the others sat on the sofa.

"Are you here to take her away?" Johnny asked Leigh, shouting from the stairs.

"No, I'm here to give her a birthday present," Leigh said. "Would you like to come over here and join us Johnny?"

"What I want is confirmation that Mackenzie is going to be staying here," Johnny responded, standing and stepping down the stairs.

"Janet Russell has that information and she will be here tomorrow to let you know," Leigh said. "Go ahead and open your present Mackenzie."

I pulled the top off the box and began pulling out the items. She had brought me ten new shirts, three pairs of pants, five pairs of shorts and two skirts. She knew I was growing out of everything very quickly, so she usually brought me new clothes each month.

"Officer Leigh, can I stay here?" I asked, after putting all the items back in the box.

"You knew this was a temporary stop over. It was just to get you comfortable in a family setting. Janet has your future in her hands. She is the one who has been talking to potential adoptive parents for you. She will let you know if anyone has chosen you and how long you have left here," Leigh informed.

"So she *is* leaving. This is such bullshit!" Johnny shouted.

"Johnny, don't worry about me. I'll be fine," I told him.

Johnny came over and sat on the floor next to me. "I'm not worried about you. I'm worried about me," he said, laying his head down in my lap.

"Johnny, just remember what we talked about. When you feel the rage burning inside, get a glass of ice water, take a few deep breaths and when you drink the water, imagine it putting out that fire. You can control your mood by putting whatever triggered your rage in the past and get over it. Each moment that passes is in the past. Change the future and you can be happy," I told him, stroking his hair.

"I don't know how I can do that without you," he told me, lifting my hand up and pressing it against his cheek.

He sat up and I reached out and embraced him. We must have held on too long because Leigh pulled us apart.

"Mackenzie, is something going on that we need to know about?" Leigh asked.

"We're friends and I've been helping him. He's been helping me. We get along and want to stay together. I want you to do for me and Johnny like you did for Angela and Gwen," I told Leigh.

"I can't promise that. He has been making progress here with Candice and Walter. There's no reason to take him from a home where he is happy and the grown-ups can handle him. Plus, Angela and Gwen were a special case. They were in danger. Johnny is not in danger here," Leigh said.

"I need her with me. Mackenzie is the reason I have been happy for a long time. She doesn't freak out and cry when I have a rage spell. There were nights we would stay up and she would tell me how great life really is when you have people around you who care for you. She cares for me and she is my only reason to have a happy life. Please don't take her from me," Johnny pleaded with Leigh.

"It's been a joy having Mackenzie here for the past couple of years, but another child might need our help. If it's time for Mackenzie to move on and go live with another family, we have to accept that," Candice told him.

"So you already know I'm leaving. I guess that means it's time for me start packing," I said, shrugging.

"Fuck that. If she goes, I go," Johnny said, heading up the stairs.

"Do you know how long I have before I leave?" I asked Leigh, accepting defeat.

"Janet will be by tomorrow to let you know. She has all that information. I'm glad that you have enjoyed your time here. Janet may decide to leave you here. I don't know what she has for you. As for now, just enjoy your birthday today. You can deal with Janet and what your future may hold tomorrow. Now, go upstairs and make sure Johnny is okay," Leigh told me.

I nodded, stood and headed up the stairs to Johnny's room. His door was closed. I pressed my ear against the door and listened for a few moments. It was eerily quiet. I knocked on his bedroom door.

"Johnny, it's Mackenzie. Can I come in?" I asked, through the door.

"Are you alone?" he asked.

"Yes, it's just me."

"Okay, you can come in."

I opened the door and saw Johnny packing his clothes into a duffle bag. I closed the door, then walked over and sat on his bed.

"What are you doing?" I asked.

"If you're leaving, then I'm leaving," he told me.

"Leigh said I may not be leaving. She said Janet has all that information and maybe she lets me stay longer like she did last year for my birthday. You've been here for a few years, it's possible I could end up staying here for years as well," I said.

"I can't take that chance. I need to be with you. I want to be ready when the time comes," he said, continuing to pack.

"Ready for what? How are you going to leave?"

"When the time is right, I have a plan. Just pack your bag and prepare to go with me."

"What do you mean with you? Where are we going?"

"We are going somewhere we can be together. You are the only girl who tried to get to know me. You actually wanted to be my friend. I've never had a real friend before and I don't want to lose the only friend and person I have ever cared about. We have to create our own family and you are my family. Go pack and I will let you know when it is time to go."

I nodded, then went to my room and sat on my bed. I didn't know what my future held for me, but I might as well prepare just in case. Johnny was right. He was my family. We had chose to stick together, no matter what and the time we had talked about was coming.

Twenty

There were nights he would sneak into my room and we would stay up most of the night talking about what would happen if Janet had found me an adoptive family. I pulled my green bag out from under my bed, placed it in front of the dresser and began packing my clothes into it. At the time, I wasn't sure if I was packing to prepare to leave with Janet, or Johnny.

Once I emptied out my dresser, I slowly and quietly made my way downstairs to get the new clothes Officer Leigh had just brought me. Halfway down the stairs, I stopped and sat down on the step, to listen to the grown-ups talk.

"Look, I'm glad Mackenzie is happy here, but Janet has found a home with people who want to adopt her," Leigh said.

"Well, that will be nice for Mackenzie to have a permanent home," Walter said.

"When Janet comes by tomorrow, she will tell you how much longer you get to spend with Mackenzie before she leaves," Leigh informed them.

I stood up and ran down the rest of the stairs, making enough noise to halt their conversation.

"How's Johnny doing?" Candice asked.

"He's fine. He just needed some space. I just came to get my new stuff to put away," I said, grabbing the box of my new clothes and quickly heading back to the stairs.

"Well, I'm going to head out. I just wanted to bring your present to you and tell you happy birthday," Leigh told me.

I set the box down on the bottom step and walked over to hug Leigh. She wrapped her arms around me and whispered in my ear.

"I hope you two aren't planning a getaway," Leigh whispered.

"No, I talked to him and everything is fine," I whispered back.

"Mackenzie, if you run away this time, I can't guarantee that you will ever be adopted. You could end up bouncing around in the system and grow up alone. You need to find a family to stay with to help you grow up successful."

"I have Johnny. He's my family. I'm going to be okay, I promise. We aren't planning anything."

I pulled away, waved to her, picked up the box and started heading back upstairs.

"Kenzie," Leigh said, after I was halfway up.

"I promise," I confirmed, even though the look on her face indicated she knew I was lying.

After hearing the grown-up's conversation, I realized I wanted to leave with Johnny. As much as I had enjoyed living in the Holmes house, I didn't want to be adopted. My mother chose to have me, then decided she didn't want me anymore. How many other people would decide they didn't want me after an undetermined period of time.

I packed my new clothes into my bag, then slid it back under the bed and walked to the next room to talk to Johnny.

"Johnny," I said, as I knocked on the door.

"Come in," Johnny said, through the door.

"So, what's the plan?" I asked, after closing the door.

"Does that mean you're in?"

"I'm in. Now tell me what you are planning."

"I'll take care of the heavy lifting. You just have your bag packed and be ready to go when I say. Are you okay with that?"

"Yes, I'm okay with that. Now can we go back downstairs and finish my birthday?"

"Okay, let's go."

Johnny and I headed downstairs to join Mr. and Mrs. Holmes for the rest of my birthday. Mrs. Holmes was slicing my cake as we entered the kitchen.

"I know we were going to watch the movie before we had cake, but how about we take the cake upstairs with us to watch the movie?" Mr. Holmes suggested.

"Yeah," Johnny and I cheered simultaneously.

We each picked up a plate with a piece of cake and a glass of milk Mr. Holmes had poured for each of us and headed upstairs. We sat in the same chair each of us had sat in every movie night and we ate our slices of cake and drank our milk while watching *Howard the Duck*.

After the movie was over, Mrs. Holmes took the plates and glasses downstairs to the kitchen while Johnny and I brushed our teeth and prepared for bed. While I washed my face, Johnny came into my room and sat on my bed. When I emerged from my bathroom, Johnny patted the bed next to him and I walked over and sat down.

"I'm going to throw your bag out the window," Johnny told me.

"Why?" I asked, as I rested my head on his shoulder.

"So when we leave, our bags are already outside," Johnny told me, wrapping his arms around me.

"So we are going to leave before Janet visits?"

"We can't take the chance that she might show up and take you with her tomorrow. We have to do this now."

"Okay, good idea."

We sat on the bed, as Johnny held me, for just a few moments before he patted me on the back and stood up. I reached down and pulled my fully packed bag out from underneath the bed. Johnny walked over and opened the window. He pushed the screen out of place and it fell straight into the bushes down below, then he picked up my bag and tossed it down into the yard.

"I will come get you, when it is time," Johnny said, as he kissed my cheek.

I was still wearing the same clothes I had on all day, so I laid down in the bed and pulled the covers up around my neck and waited for Mr. and Mrs. Holmes to come in and tell me good night.

I laid on my back and stared up at the ceiling. I trusted Johnny to have a plan, but knew that he was more impulsive rather than pre-meditative. When I heard mom and dad Holmes heading up the stairs, I grabbed the edge of the blanket and held it tight around my neck.

"Good night Mackenzie. Officer Leigh said that Mrs. Russell will stop by tomorrow and let us know how much time we have left with you," Candice told me.

"I know, I heard Officer Leigh say earlier that I am going to be adopted," I admitted.

"Were you being sneaky and eavesdropping on our conversation?" Walter asked.

"I was coming downstairs to get my present and I heard y'all talking. I just wanted to know where I was going," I said.

"Well, get some sleep and we will see you in the morning," Candice said, after they kissed me on the forehead.

Mr. and Mrs. Holmes left the room and I waited for Johnny. As I laid there, I thought about where we were going to live and how we were going to eat. At some point, I began to doze off.

When Johnny came into my room, he patted my shoulder and shook me slightly to get my attention. I slowly blinked my eyes open as he pulled the covers down off me. He was fully dressed and he tossed his bag out the window.

"So, are we going to sneak out the window, or are we going out the front door?" I asked.

"It depends on how fast you can out run the fire," he told me.

"What do you mean, out run the fire?"

"I closed your door because it is meant to hold off the fire from getting in here. I set a fire in my room."

"Why did you do that?" I asked.

"If you can't live here, then no one can. Let's go," Johnny told me.

"What about mom and dad?"

"They will be fine. Their bedroom door is closed. Hurry before the smoke detectors go off," he said, ushering me toward the window.

As the smoke began seeping under the door, I allowed him to help me out the window. We scaled down the trellis, into the backyard where our bags were waiting.

Johnny picked up both bags, slung them over his shoulder and grabbed my hand. He rushed me away from the house. As we reached the edge of the yard, I turned to look at the house. There was an orange glow flickering from the window of the bedroom Johnny had stayed in.

"Come on, we've got to get out of here before anyone notices," Johnny said, pulling on my arm.

"What about mom and dad? I want to make sure they get out okay," I told him.

"They are grown-ups. They can get out by themselves. Besides, I made sure they were still awake before I set the fire. Now let's go," Johnny said, opening the gate that led out to a large field behind the house.

Johnny kept us covered by the shadows until we made it out to the main road. It was only a few moments before we heard the fire truck sirens. We continued walking until Johnny walked down behind a strip center.

"We can camp here until morning," Johnny said, pulling blankets out of his bag and setting up a sleeping space behind a dumpster.

"Is this a good idea? I can call Officer Leigh and we can stay at her house," I suggested.

"If you call her, we could be in trouble."

"Why would we be in trouble?"

"I set a fire in the house and both of us made it out safely with all our stuff. We will be charged with arson and will go to kid jail."

"Okay, so what do we do now?" I asked.

"We stay here for the night and in the morning, we can go as far away from here as we want," Johnny told me.

"What do we do for money?"

"Don't worry about that. I'll take care of it."

Johnny sat down on the make shift bed and leaned against the dumpster. I looked around, not seeing anyone, then sat down next to him and cuddled into be crook of his arm. He wrapped his arms around me and I somehow managed to eventually fall asleep.

Twenty One

The next morning, Johnny woke me up just as the sun was peeking over the horizon. He nudged me in the back with his shoulder.

"Where can I go to the bathroom? I need to pee," I said, as he hooked his hands under my arms and pushed me into a standing position.

"There is a place around the corner we can go to, or you can go right here behind the dumpster," Johnny said, standing up and folding the blankets we slept on.

"Ewe, I can't pee outside. First of all, I don't have the right equipment and second, I need toilet paper."

"Don't be such a girl. If you squat just right, you can do it and as for the toilet paper, I'm sure I can find something for you to use. If you have to go, just go. You don't want to hold it in until you pee your pants."

"Okay, fine. Only because as we are talking about it, I really have to go and can't wait."

I stepped behind the dumpster where I wouldn't be seen and did the best I could to not pee all over myself. As I finished, Johnny's hand appeared with a napkin. I finished and pulled my pants back up, then re-emerged to where he was waiting for me in front of the dumpster.

"Toss the napkin in the trash and grab your bag. We need to get moving," Johnny told me.

I tossed the napkin, picked up my bag, slung it over my shoulder, then followed behind him as he made sure we could travel without rousing alarm. Luckily, it was still early and there weren't too many cars out on the road.

"Where are we going?" I asked.

"There is a state park we can go to. It's large enough to where we can camp without being noticed," he told me.

It took us two weeks to make it all the way to the state park. I didn't know where Johnny got our food from, but he made sure we had three meals a day. He had somehow procured a tent for us after a couple of days that we were able to use as shelter at night and any time it rained.

In those two weeks, Johnny never had a rage episode and he made sure to make it seem like an adventure. We played games, like hide and don't get caught, whenever we saw a police car. When we had finally arrived at the state park, we sat down on a bench over looking a historical monument and decided it was a good place to eat lunch.

"We are going to need to go far into the wooded area in order to keep from being noticed," Johnny told me, as we had finished eating.

Just as we were packing up and getting ready to head into the woods, a park ranger came by on foot and stopped in front of us.

"Where are your parents?" he asked.

"Oh, they are camping near by. My sister and I decided to take a walk and just happened to stop for a bite to eat," Johnny tried lying to him.

"I doubt that. Come on, let's go back to the office," the park ranger said, knowing Johnny had made up a story.

We followed the park ranger up to the front of the state park where the tourist center was. When we walked through the door, the park ranger motioned to a couple of chairs.

"Have a seat. I'm going to call someone to come get you two," he told us.

"We can still run. I know if we go right out that door, we can get to the woods and hide," Johnny said, as the park ranger called the police.

"It took us two weeks to get here. How much longer are we going to have to run before we are caught again?" I asked him, nervously.

"Okay, I'm just trying to protect you. I want us to stay together. If the police come to get us, we will most definitely be separated," Johnny said, lightly touching the side of my face.

"Besides that, our pictures are right there on the wall. That's how the ranger knew you were lying," I informed him, pointing at a missing poster tacked up to a bulletin board on the wall behind the welcome desk.

"Well shit. I wish I would have known that when he approached us. I would have grabbed you and we would have run away from him when he approached."

"That wouldn't have solved the problem. We still would have eventually been caught."

"Only because you are wanted. If I had left by my-self, no one would have come looking for me."

"That's not true Johnny. Plus, I thought we ran away together so we could be together," I said, holding his hand.

"Well, now we aren't going to be together. They are going to take you to your new home and I'm going to a juvenile detention center," Johnny said.

"I'll talk to Officer Leigh and see what she can do for you."

"You must be one special little girl. They are send-ing a specific officer to come get you," the park ranger said, as he emerged around from behind the desk.

"Shit, Officer Leigh is coming to get us," I said, lowering my head and resting it in my free hand.

As we waited, Johnny and I just sat quietly, holding on to each other. When Officer Leigh showed up to get us, I was confused by her reaction.

"Oh honey, you had me so worried," Officer Leigh said, hugging me.

"You're not mad at me?" I asked her.

"I'm just glad you're okay. Johnny, are you okay?" Leigh wondered, checking both of us for injuries.

"I kept her safe," was all Johnny said.

"Thank you, sir. I appreciate you saving the chil-dren," Leigh said to the park ranger.

"Please ma'am, call me Barry," the ranger told her.

"Okay, Barry. I'm going to be taking the kids with me. Do I need to sign any papers that show I came to get them?" Leigh asked.

"No ma'am. I didn't fill out any paperwork because on the phone I was told someone was coming right away. I didn't think I needed to."

"Don't worry. I'll send over a police report and get your statement."

"Are we going to jail?" Johnny asked Leigh.

"No, you're not going to jail. I'm going to take you to the police station, so we can find out what happened," Leigh responded.

"I'm glad that I was able to assist the police with finding these children," Barry said, pulling the missing poster down off the bulletin board.

"Thank you, Barry. Okay kids, let's go," Officer Leigh said, after shaking Barry's hand and proceeded to usher us out to the car.

Johnny and I sat next to each other in the back seat of Leigh's car, holding hands. Leigh periodically peered at us in the rear view mirror and Johnny would look over at me, squeezing my hand.

"When I grow up, I will find you again," Johnny whispered to me.

I smiled at him when we arrived at the police station. Officer Leigh parked the car, then took us inside and walked up to another officer.

"Bailey, are you able to take Johnny Taylor into another room and get his statement?" Leigh asked the other officer.

"Sure thing, Leigh. Come on, son. I need you to come with me," Bailey said, addressing Johnny.

"I'm not going anywhere without Mackenzie," Johnny said, wrapping his arms around me and holding on just a little too tight.

"Johnny, you're hurting me," I said, trying to wriggle out of his grasp.

"I'm so sorry, Mackenzie. Please don't be mad at me," he said, loosening his grip.

"I'm not mad Johnny. Look, all we have to do, is go into two separate rooms and give our account of what happened and what we have been doing since the fire. I promise I will come see you before we leave here," I told him, placing my hands on his face.

Johnny nodded, then he kissed me on my forehead before we were separated and placed into different rooms. I sat at a table with a notepad and pen in front of me. I kept my hands in my lap and waited. After a few moments, Leigh joined me in the room and sat across the table from me.

"Tell me what happened Mackenzie," Leigh requested.

I didn't want to get Johnny into trouble, so all I said was, "he kept me safe."

"Johnny already admitted to setting the fire. I just want to know how you fit into this. Did you help him set the fire so you two could run away together?" Leigh asked.

"I didn't set the fire. Johnny kept me safe from the fire," I told her. "What's going to happen to us now?"

"Well, since Johnny admitted to setting the fire, he can't go back to live with Mr. and Mrs. Holmes. We are going to need to find another placement for him, even if that means he spends a few months in a juvenile detention center. The family that you were supposed to go live with, has changed their mind. They had thought about adopting you and have now decided that you are a dangerous risk. Now Janet has found you another temporary foster home to stay in until she can find you permanent housing."

"So what else is new? I've spent the last few years in temporary housing. What's a few more years going to hurt?" I said.

"Mackenzie, you need to embrace the family life if you plan to survive the system," Leigh told me.

"I had a family, but I was being ripped away from them. Johnny was just trying to hold on to the one person he could count on for the rest of his life, me. We had each other, but we wouldn't be able to stay together. I don't know how long I will stay at any house, so I think from now on, I'm going to keep to myself."

"Mackenzie, all you need to do is be gracious to the family who takes you in and you could end up staying with a family you like for a long time," Leigh said.

"That is until a family decides they want to adopt me and I'm taken from another good family that I get along with," I said, emphatically slamming my hand down on the table.

"Well, I can assure you that Janet will no longer suggest you to a potential adoption. You can go to a foster home with the option for adoption, but that is the only way she will be able to get you adopted now. It's in your file that you are a potential risk for running away, so it is less likely that anyone will select you."

"Fuck it, I don't care," I said, leaning back in my seat and crossing my arms over my chest.

"Mackenzie, watch your mouth. What happened to the sweet girl I first met?"

"I'm learning to take care of myself. No one is ever going to tell me what to do ever again. One day I will find someone like Johnny who loves me and chooses to be my family. If you decide that you want to be that mother figure for me, then be there for me. If I ask you to protect me, then protect me. If I tell you I am happy somewhere, leave me there. There is no reason to remove me from a home where I am being well taken care of, just to place me into a home where I have to start all over again. That girl from all those years ago is gone," I told her.

"Well Mackenzie, I hope that sweet girl comes back and I get to see her again," Leigh said.

"Good luck with that. I don't know if she will ever be back."

"Janet should be here soon. She has a new home for you to go to."

"Of course she does. What about Candice and Walter Holmes? Are they okay?"

"Yes, they are fine. They were able to escape the house before the entire top floor was engulfed in flames. Luckily, the fire department arrived very quickly and the fire only took their second story. There is minimal work that needs to be done to the first floor before it is livable again, but for now they are staying in a motel."

"So where am I going next?"

"Janet has that information. I have been looking for you the past two weeks and she has been trying to find you new placement. She should be here within the hour to take you there. If you want to see Johnny before you go, now is your chance," Leigh said, walking over to the door and placing her hand on the door knob.

I stood up as she opened the door. I followed the officer through the station and toward the back area where I had never been before. There was a room surrounded by windows, with holes strategically placed for air and had two benches. Johnny was sitting, hunched over, on one of the benches. His elbows were on his knees and his face was in his hands. He looked like an animal in a cage.

"Johnny," I said, standing in front of one of the air holes.

"Mackenzie?" he said, slowly lifting his head.

Officer Leigh opened the door to the room and let me go in with him. I rushed over and sat on the bench in front of him. He was facing my direction, but he seemed to be looking through me.

"Johnny, look at me."

"Mackenzie, I'm going to jail for kids. What's gonna happen to me?" he said, reaching out and touching my hand.

"It's only going to be a few months, then they are going to find you another home. You aren't going to be there long," I told him.

"How do you know that?"

"Officer Leigh told me."

"She doesn't really know either. In order for me to get out, I have to be able to control my anger."

"Johnny, you can do this. Just keep to yourself while you are there and eventually you will be able to get out."

"What about you? Will I ever see you again?"

"I promise I will find you again one day," I reassured him.

"Come on Mackenzie. Janet is here for you," Officer Leigh said.

"Don't worry Johnny. We will find each other again one day," I told him, standing.

Johnny stood up and wrapped his arms around me. I fell into his embrace.

Twenty Two

Johnny was carted off and I was placed in a room to wait for Janet Russell to take me to my next foster home. Knowing that Johnny and I were being separated anyway, I couldn't figure out why he chose to run away for two weeks, rather than just spending those two weeks together in the nice home that Mr. and Mrs. Holmes had provided for us.

"Well, let's hope you get along with the couple at the next home," Janet said, as she entered the room.

"So, who are they?" I asked, standing up.

"Grace and Richard Perry. They have four of their own children who have since grown up and moved out. They have grandchildren who come to stay with them on a regular basis, so you will have someone to play with sometimes," Janet Russell said, as we walked out to her car.

"So I'm back to being the lone child in the house? Why don't they foster more than one at a time," I asked.

"They feel as though because they are getting older, it's easier for them to focus on one child at a time. Now, the girls that stay at their home tend to stay a little longer than the boys, so you could end up staying with them for a while."

"Great, so Mrs. Perry could turn out to be another Betty Warren. Is there anything weird about them I should know about?" I wondered.

"Grace is nothing like Mrs. Warren. She enjoys taking care of the children in her house. What do you mean by weird? Weird how?" Janet wanted to know.

"Are there any stories about the other children in their home having problems?"

"Nothing that I was informed of. According to their file, depending on their age, the boys generally stay for about six months. At that time, Mr. Perry begins to accuse them of being attracted to his wife and he thinks it is in their best interest to leave. Mrs. Perry denies the claims as well as the boys. The girls usually stay between two and three years. For some reason, which is not noted in their file, when the girls turn thirteen, they become uncontrollable teenagers."

"Well, I guess we will find out what is causing these girls to become uncontrollable. Have they had any foster kids that have stayed with them until they aged out of the system?"

"A few, but more often than not, Mr. and Mrs. Perry return the kids to the system with an excuse as to why they couldn't handle them anymore."

"Wonderful. Well, let's go meet them," I said, as Janet pulled up to my next foster home.

The home was older and the lawn needed to be tended to. Grace Perry was an overweight plain woman with short brown hair, oily skin and a few missing teeth. Richard Perry had thinning hair on top of his head, but with the hair he had left, spanning around the back of his head from ear to ear, he was in desperate need of a hair cut. With his large wire rimmed glasses, his gaze gave me the heebie jeebies.

"Mr. and Mrs. Perry, this is Mackenzie Leigh. She's had a rough few years, so we are hoping she will be comfortable here," Janet said, as we sat on a very warn brown sofa in their living room.

"I'm sure she will be very happy here," Mr. Perry said, licking and sucking his front top teeth as he glared at me.

"Mrs. Perry, how about you show me to the room I will be staying in," I said, wanting to get away from Richard and his creepy stare.

"Sure," Grace said, standing up and taking my hand.

I picked up my bag and slung it over my shoulder. She led me down a hallway and into a bedroom with a mattress on the floor. The room was empty otherwise, but I didn't mind living out of my bag as long as I wasn't there for too long. The walls were stained with a dark colored substance smeared from about waist high down to the base boards. I tossed my bag into a corner, then turned to face Grace, who stood in the hallway.

"Where is your room?" I asked Grace.

"Right next door. In case you need anything, we are close by," she told me, looking down the hallway into the living room.

"Did you get her settled in?" Richard said, loudly from the living room.

"Yes sir," Grace responded.

I was confused as I followed Mrs. Perry back down the hallway and we returned to the living room. I had never heard a woman call her husband sir. Both Mr. Perry and Janet Russell stood as we rejoined them.

"Okay Mackenzie, I'm going to leave you to it. I'll be back in a month to check on you," Janet said, heading for the door.

I waved as she left, then turned toward Mr. and Mrs. Perry. Grace was standing behind Richard peeking at me over his shoulder. Richard stood over me, staring down into my eyes.

"How old are you?" he asked.

"Eleven," I responded.

"That's perfect. We might need to get you some new clothes once the first foster check comes in," he said, licking and sucking his top front teeth again.

"I have clothes," I told him.

"Yes, I can see that. The only problem is they aren't very flattering on you," he remarked.

"Whatever, I'm hungry. Can I have a snack?" I said, ignoring him.

"I'll make you a sandwich," Grace said, skittering off to the kitchen.

The first few months in the Perry house were very awkward for me. Mr. Perry took me shopping for clothes and chose quite a few outfits that I felt were very inappropriate. He also insisted I wear a bra, even though I hadn't developed enough.

He had me try on the clothes at the store to make sure they fit, but as soon as we got home, Mr. Perry wanted me to model the clothes for him. He sat down in his chair in the living room and Mrs. Perry was instructed to sit at the table in the dining room with her back to the living room.

I took the shopping bags into the room I slept in and changed into the first outfit. I put on a pair of shorts that were so short my butt cheeks were peeking out the bottom and a V neck tank top that had such a deep V, I felt almost naked.

"Come on out here beautiful and let me see," Mr. Perry said, as I poked my head out of the bedroom door and looked down the hall.

I stepped out and walked into the living room. When I stopped in from of him, he let out a very uncomfortable moan. He motioned for me to turn around in a complete circle and I complied. He moaned until I made it back around to face him.

"Oh, that's a good one. I like that. I'm glad you didn't put the bra on with this shirt. It's better this way," he said, licking and sucking his teeth as he looked me up and down.

He leaned forward and grabbed my hand. I took a step back when he tried pulling me toward him. Mr. Perry pulled harder and I stumbled forward. He grabbed my hips so I couldn't get away and forced me to sit on his lap. I tried to get up, but he wrapped his arms around me so tight, I gave in.

"You are such a pretty girl. You should really wear more clothes that show off your developing body," he told me, as he smelled my hair.

I just sat on his lap, quietly and didn't move. When I had first arrived and he had me sit on his lap, if I moved, he moaned.

"Okay beautiful, show me the bra," he told me, turning me so my legs were between his knees, but held onto my hips so I couldn't stand up right away.

He moaned one more time before releasing me and I ran back to the room. I fell onto the mattress and cried until he yelled for me to come out and show him the bra. I took a deep breath, wiped my face, put the bra on, then put on another deep V neck tank top he had purchased for me.

I re-emerged into the hallway and started walking toward the living room. As I stepped out of the hallway, he held up his hand to stop me.

"Why are you wearing that shirt? I wanted to see the bra. Take it off," he said, leaning back into his chair. I turned to walk back to the room and he yelled, "that's not what I said. Do it right here. Take off your shirt right here, slowly."

I lowered my head, crossed my arms in front of my body and grabbed the bottom of the shirt. Complying with his request, I slowly lifted my shirt up over my head. Once I was exposed, I held the shirt in front of my chest.

"Come over here beautiful. Stand in front of me," he requested.

I again complied and walked over to stand in front of him. He reached up and took the shirt from me, then pulled me into his lap again. He held me as if I were a toddler who had just climbed up into daddy's lap. Mr. Perry placed his hand on the side of my head and forced me to lay my head down on his shoulder.

"Grace, get me the television clicker. It's family T.V. time. You can join us now," he said to Mrs. Perry.

"Yes sir," Mrs. Perry said, jumping up from the dining room table and scrambling to get him the remote to the television.

I laid in Mr. Perry's lap while he drank a couple of beers and watched a crude comedic movie. A couple of times I tried to get up, but he tightened his grip on me, so I stayed in the position until he carried me to my room. He placed me on the mattress and laid down next to me.

I then laid on the mattress with him cuddled up behind me. I cried quietly, while he wrapped his arm around me and pulled me close against him.

"Okay you two, dinner is ready," Mrs. Perry called from the kitchen.

"Get dressed for dinner and we'll wait for you," Mr. Perry said, slowly running the back of his fingers down my arm before getting up and leaving the room.

I changed into jeans and a t-shirt, went to the bathroom to wash my face, before heading out to the dining room. Mr. and Mrs. Perry sat on opposite ends of the table, like always and I sat on the side, closest to Mr. Perry. He insisted I sit close to him.

Every night Mr. Perry would come into my room and lay down on the mattress and cuddle me. He would hold on to me so tight each night, I was unable to move, or get up.

On my twelfth birthday, Officer Leigh came to visit me and gave me my birthday present, just like she always did every year. I was so glad to see her every time she came to visit because that meant I wouldn't have to listen to Mr. Perry make comments about how my body was developing and I didn't have to sit on his lap.

"Hey Mackenzie. Happy birthday," Officer Leigh said, as I walked down the hallway from the bedroom to the living room.

"Please tell me you didn't buy me clothes this time," I said, sighing.

"Actually, no. You are growing into a young woman and I wanted to bring you something you could keep with you for the rest of your life," she told me, handing me a box as I sat on the sofa. "How are you getting along here?"

"Mackenzie and I are best buddies, aren't we?" Mr. Perry said, sitting down next to me on the sofa and putting his arm around my shoulders.

"Sure, you could say that," I said, trying to wriggle away from his touch, but he tightened his grip on my shoulder.

"That's good to hear. I'm so glad you are happy here," Officer Leigh said, as if not to raise suspicion that she knew something was wrong. "Open your present."

I nodded and leaned forward to release my shoulders from Mr. Perry's grip. I removed the lid on the box and pulled out a photo of Officer Leigh and me that had been taken the day she rescued me. I was sitting in the dirty chair next to her desk and she was knelt down in front of me. It appeared as though I was crying and she was trying to reassure me. The photo had been placed in a wooden frame that appeared to be handmade. The word *Family* had been scrawled along the bottom of the frame with a permanent marker.

"Who took this picture?" I asked.

"Officer Bailey did," Leigh told me.

"I didn't even know anyone had taken this photo," I said, tears filling my eyes.

"Neither did I. When I was recently promoted to detective, he presented the photo to me as a congratulations. I made the frame and thought you would like it," she told me.

"I love it," I said, lunging across the room and wrapping my arms around her.

"Lunch is ready for the birthday girl," Mrs. Perry said, in a sing song way from the kitchen.

"Well, that's my cue to go," Officer Leigh said, standing to leave.

"No, you could stay for lunch," I said, keeping my arms wrapped around her waist.

Mr. Perry loudly cleared his throat and snapped his fingers. I immediately let go of Leigh and stepped back to stand next to him. I lowered my head and looked at my feet.

"Now Mackenzie, a big important detective, like Leigh here, probably has more important things to do," Richard said, pulling me over to stand in front of him and enveloping both his arms tight around my shoulders in order to hold my arms down.

"You know the drill. Janet will be by tomorrow to check on you," Leigh informed, as she walked toward the front door and left.

Mr. Perry pressed himself against my back and led me into the dining room as soon as Leigh closed the door behind her. He pulled my chair out for me and I sat down. He normally sat at the head of the table, but that time, he sat in the chair right next to me and placed his hand on my thigh.

That night, when Mr. Perry came into my bedroom, he got a little handsy with me. I tried to pretend I was asleep, but he knew I wasn't when I flinched as he placed his hand on my bottom.

Every time when Janet Russell came to visit, I wasn't allowed to be alone in the room with her, Richard was always there. His nighttime visits made me very uncomfortable and each time he talked to me in a soothing tone, as if it would make what he was doing to me more relaxing.

"I won't be around tomorrow when Mrs. Russell comes to visit, but you need to keep our special time our secret. Besides, no one would believe you anyway," he told me one night, before leaving my bedroom.

It had been several months of his touchy feely nighttime visits and I wasn't even sure what I would say to Janet. When she showed up, Grace stayed close by to make sure I didn't say anything and Janet was only there for about ten minutes.

Leigh came to visit me two weeks later and became even more suspicious that something was wrong with me. I was quiet and barely spoke to her.

"Mackenzie, you sure are quiet today," Leigh said, while Richard sat right next to me on the sofa with his arm around my shoulders, again.

"She's in that preteen stage. She barely talks to anyone these days," Mr. Perry answered for me.

"Mackenzie, why don't you walk me to my car?" she suggested, standing and extending her hand to me.

I slowly reached out to grab her hand, but Mr. Perry pulled it back and patted my shoulder. He looked over at me as I stared at my lap.

"Daddy, is it okay if I go out to the car with Miss Leigh?" I asked him, without looking up.

"Sure sweetheart. Just remember," he started aloud, before whispering in my ear. "Don't tell her our secret."

He kissed me on my cheek, then loosened his grip around my shoulders. I stood up and slowly walked toward the front door, looking at the floor the whole way, where Leigh was waiting for me. We stepped outside and Leigh closed the door.

"What is going on Mackenzie?" Leigh asked, as we walked toward her car.

I turned around and glanced back at the front window of the house. Richard was watching us through the window. He held one finger vertically just below his nose. I turned back around and watched my feet move one in front of the other until we made it to her car.

"I'm not supposed to tell you," I informed her.

"Mackenzie, is Mr. Perry hurting you?"

"Sometimes it hurts, but other times I'm just uncomfortable."

"Uncomfortable how?"

"He comes into my room at night and does stuff to me," I told her, sitting down on the curb in front of her car.

"How long has this been happening?" she asked, sitting on the curb next to me.

"When I first got here, I slept in my bed alone for only two weeks, then he started sleeping in the bed with me. At first he would just hold me while we slept, but after my birthday he started touching me in places I didn't want him to. This is every night."

"Have you said anything to Janet?"

"No, he never leaves me alone with her. I'm surprised he even allowed me out here with you alone."

"Well, I tell you this much, you are NOT going back into that house."

"I don't want him to get mad. Please don't tell him I told you," I pleaded, crying.

"Don't worry, I won't alert him," she assured me, touching my hand.

I abruptly recoiled away from her, which caused her to become angry. She began taking deep breaths as if to calm her anger. Leigh stood up and walked around to the driver's side of her car. She opened the door and reached in, retrieving her police radio.

"Attention all units in the vicinity of Union and Runway, this is Detective Leigh. I'm going to need back up. Child in danger at a foster home," Leigh said, into her CB mic.

"10-4 detective. This is unit 237 responding. Arrival time, three minutes," came a response over the CB radio.

"10-4 unit 237. I'm outside the residence with the victim," Leigh responded.

"10-4."

Leigh replaced the mic into her car and returned to my side on the curb. She started to reach her arm around me, but I whimpered like a wounded animal and moved away from her. She put her arm down and placed it in her lap.

"I am so sorry sweet girl," she told me, as the police car rounded the corner without the siren on and stopped in front of Leigh's car. Two officers emerged and approached us as we stood up.

"Whatever that little bitch said to you, she's a liar," Richard yelled, as he appeared in the open doorway to the house.

"Sir, let's go inside and talk," the officer that was driving the patrol car told him.

"That was supposed to be our secret Mackenzie. I thought we were friends," Richard continued to yell, as the officer attempted to get him back into the house.

"Mackenzie, this is Officer Samuels. She is going to sit with you while I go inside and gather your belongings," Leigh told me, introducing the officer that had exited the patrol car on the passenger side.

"No, please don't leave me," I pleaded with Leigh.

"Okay, Samuels, can you please go inside and have Mrs. Perry show you to Mackenzie's room and bring her things out here. I'm going to take her back to my house and contact Janet Russell, her social worker, from there," Leigh instructed.

Officer Samuels nodded and headed up to the house. I clung to Leigh, not wanting to let go. I pressed one ear against Leigh's shoulder, as she pressed her hand against my other ear, so I couldn't hear Richard Perry yelling from his living room.

After a few moments, Leigh began moving me toward her car and opened the door to her back seat. I climbed into the car and laid down across the seat. I pressed my hands against my ears when I heard Richard Perry's yelling become louder and louder.

"You stupid fucking bitch. I will kill you for telling our secret," Richard yelled, before I could no longer hear him.

I assumed he had been placed in the back seat of the patrol car, but I didn't want to look. I felt the car rock as the trunk was closed and Leigh climbed in behind the steering wheel.

I fell asleep in the back seat of Leigh's car, as she drove to her house. When we arrived she reached to the back and shook me slightly to rouse me. I screamed at the top of my voice from her touch.

"Mackenzie, I'm sorry. It's okay. You're okay. Let's go inside," Leigh said, when I opened my eyes and stopped screaming.

She left my bag in the trunk of her car as we went inside. I strolled over to the sofa and laid down, while Leigh called Janet Russell.

"Janet, this is Detective Leigh. Can you meet me at my house? I have Mackenzie here with me. I'll explain when you get here. No, she is safe now and Mr. Perry has been arrested. Mackenzie needs a new home. Okay, see you soon," Leigh said, before hanging up the phone.

"Is she going to find me a new home to stay in or can I finally stay with you?" I asked.

"I don't know. She's going to come over and talk for now."

"I'm tired. Can I take a nap in my old room until she gets here?"

"Of course you can. I'll come get you if she wants to talk to you, or has a new home lined up for you."

Twenty Three

Janet Russell decided that it was okay for me to spend a few months at Leigh's house. I stayed with Leigh until after the Christmas holiday.

"Are you ready to go to your new foster home to-day?" Leigh asked, as we ate breakfast together for the last time.

"Not really. I've enjoyed it here. You know, when I was six and kept begging to live with you, you said I couldn't because your job was too demanding. Even Janet said no because of your job. Why was I able to stay here these past few months?"

"Well, you remember I was promoted from officer to detective?"

"Yeah."

"That detective position came with a desk job. I investigate crimes against children and you helped me get that position. I'm no longer on the streets risking my life everyday. I help children who have been abused to get out of their abusive homes and I assist social services with investigating new potential foster parents.

"Janet decided since you were comfortable with me, it would be best to keep you with me until she could find you a new home to go to. Plus, you are older and can practically take care of yourself," Leigh explained.

"Okay, so if that's the case now, why don't I just stay here with you?" I wondered.

"You need to interact with other children in your situation. I'm also hoping to go further in my career. I want to help place children in good homes. If I housed all the children I felt a connection with, my house would be full of kids. You need to find a home with other children and choose your family."

"What do you mean, choose my family?"

"Think about it this way. You can be fed and grow up in a home, but once you hit a certain age, you will move out and probably never see the foster parents again. If you connect with another child in the foster care system and live in the same house with them, when y'all grow up, you will have a pre-made family with someone that you actually chose to be with."

"What if I said I choose to live with you?"

"Mackenzie, please don't make this any harder than it has to be. In order for me to become an official foster parent there are several classes I have to take and an investigation will be done on my life. I just prefer not to have people prying into my life. Can we please just leave it there?"

"Fine, I guess we should get going, so I can start choosing my family as soon as possible," I told her, placing my breakfast plate into the sink.

I walked back to my room, changed my clothes, packed up my bag and walked back out to the living room. Leigh was finishing washing the breakfast dishes when I dropped my bag on the floor. I walked over and sat on one of the bar stools.

"So where am I going?" I asked her, as she wiped her hands on a dish towel after putting away the last clean dish.

"Mrs. Russell found you a group home to stay in. There are a lot of other children there. Some of them have spent time in juvenile detention centers, but since you got along with Johnny so well, she thought you would fit in with them," Leigh said, as we walked out to her car and I tossed my bag in the back seat.

"Please tell me you have investigated this group home," I inquired, as she drove.

"Yes, I did. The foster parents like to house older children who can learn to take care of themselves because they work from home, so they are always there, but not always available. Most of the kids in their care have troubled backgrounds and tend to get into trouble with the law. With them being home all the time, it has stopped the children from committing crimes and keeps them on the straight and narrow," Leigh explained.

"Do you know if Johnny could be there?" I wondered.

"No sweetie, he's not. Johnny was actually adopted by the same couple that adopted Angela and Gwen. He is safe and hasn't caused anymore problems. Of course, he spent six months in the detention center before being requested for adoption."

"Well that's good. I'm glad to hear that. So this group home is similar to the foster care facility?"

"I guess you could say that. You are basically taught to take care of yourself and you are homeschooled. The couple has a personal chef and one of your classes is a cooking class with the personal chef. The house is large enough to be a hotel. There are several children in each room to keep you all from being lonely."

"How nice. Forget an actual family setting, let's cram the kids all in one bedroom so they won't be lonely," I said, sarcastically.

"Mackenzie, you need to bond with someone so you can have a family outside of the system," Leigh said.

"You mean like Johnny?"

"Would you stop. The Holmes couple only took in short term foster kids. Johnny was a special case. Not only that, but they no longer foster children anymore."

"Why not?"

"They really liked you and Johnny and enjoyed being a family together, but since Johnny set fire to their home, they don't want to risk it. They have moved out to a large piece of property with a small home and now they foster animals."

"Well ain't that a bitch."

"My goodness Mackenzie. Every house you go to, your personality changes. Hopefully, this group home will bring back that sweet girl," Leigh said.

"I doubt it," I said, crossing my arms over my chest.

"Well, I'm glad that what Richard Perry did to you was easily reversible and you're back to my sassy preteen."

We pulled up to a large home that I agreed looked like a hotel. The lawn was manicured and the outside of the home was pristine. Before we were able to exit the vehicle, a large group of children came running out of the home, laughing. They scattered throughout the yard and played.

"Well, looks like it could be fun here," Leigh observed.

"Sure, I could give it a try. Let's hope this is the end," I said, sighing.

We got out of the car and I reached into the back seat and grabbed my bag. Heading up toward the front door, we passed the other children.

"Fresh meat," yelled one teenage boy.

"Whoo, whoo," another teenage boy cat called.

"Great, now I have to worry about the other kids," I said to Leigh, just as she knocked on the door.

"Don't worry about them. Their bark is worse than their bite. They yell things, but don't actually act on anything. I'm Jojo. I'm fourteen years old. What's your name?" a boy, who was sitting alone at a table on the porch, said.

"I'm Mackenzie. I'm twelve," I responded.

"Come on. I'll take you inside. Tim and Margaret are working and probably won't come to the door. The maid is upstairs tending to the rooms and the chef doesn't answer the door," Jojo said, opening the door and allowing Leigh and I go in ahead of him.

Just inside the front door was a large open area that looked like a hotel lobby. Approximately fifty feet from the front door was a wall with a swinging door smack dab in the middle. There was a hallway down the left side of the wall and a hallway down the right side of the wall.

"Is there any way I could speak with Tim or Margaret?" Leigh asked him.

"If you want. I can show Mackenzie to the dorms and Tim's office is down the hallway on the left and

Margaret's office is down the hallway on the right," Jojo told her.

"Are you going to be okay Mackenzie?" Leigh asked.

"I'm fine," I told her.

"Okay, I'll see you later," she said, heading for the hallway to the right.

"So, that swinging door right there, that's the kitchen. Now, if we go upstairs I can show you the dorms. There are three floors of dorm rooms. All of the rooms are set up the same way. There are six beds in each room - three sets of bunk beds. Once one bed is vacated, it is soon filled. The rooms are mixed both boys and girls, but the bathrooms are split," Jojo told me as we headed up the stairs.

"Is there a free bed in your room?" I wondered.

"As a matter of fact, there is. The bed right next to mine is open. Come on, I'll show you."

Jojo took me up to the third floor and into the second room at the top of the stairs. All of the beds were made and the room was clean and clear of clutter.

"You have the choice of unpacking your bag and putting your items in the footlocker, or you can just put your bag in the footlocker and pick out of it," he told me, referring to what looked like a treasure chest at the foot of each bed.

"What do you do with your things?" I asked him.

"I unpacked my bag when I got here last year because all I had was a trash bag that my clothes were crammed into. I have lived like a hobo for most of my life."

"Well then, I guess I will unpack my things and use the footlocker."

I smiled at him and he smiled back. I was so glad to find someone I connected with. He turned the key that was hanging from the lock in the front of the footlocker and opened the chest for me. I placed my bag down on the floor in front of the footlocker and began to unpack what few clothes I had.

"Alright Mac, let's go outside with the other kids and enjoy this nice day," Jojo said, assigning me a nickname.

Jojo and I were basically inseparable. Most nights we would sneak out of the house and galavant around the property. If we ended up getting caught, Tim would come outside and let us know we were not allowed back in the house for the night. Since we had gone out the window in our bedroom, we would go back in through that window.

By the time we would get back into the room and into our beds, we only had a couple of hours of sleep before Tim and Margaret would come in each room to wake us up for classes. Jojo was the only one who called me Mac. It was as if he had a pet name for me. I was completely enamored with him. For a full year we did everything together.

We eventually decided to be a couple and kissed a few times. I loved him and I was sure he loved me too. Sometimes we would climb up into his bed and he would hold me all night while we slept. I always felt safe with his arms wrapped around me.

I was so glad that Tim pretty much stayed away from the girls and we only really interacted with Margaret. Jojo and I mostly only interacted with each other. He kept me safe from the sixteen and seventeen year old boys who thought it was funny to grab the developing girls inappropriately.

A couple of months after he turned fifteen and four months after I turned thirteen, Tim and Margaret decided that they could no longer deal with the two of us together. They contacted social services who sent a couple to the group home looking for a troubled older child to adopt. They were specific in wanting a boy.

After looking through all of the files and meeting the boys, they chose Jojo. Despite him being unwilling to follow rules, he still respected authority. He lived with the idea that you only get the same amount of respect that you give.

I was devastated. He was going to be leaving me and I was feeling apprehensive about living in the group home without him. He was the one who saved me from my nightmares. I would relive the abuse from all the foster homes I had been in before. I felt as though I had found a place I could actually call home and someone I could call family, but it would soon be taken away from me.

A couple of weeks after he was chosen, Jojo moved out of the group home. I tried keeping to myself, but one of the older boys, Adam, in the room decided to claim me. He forced me to be with him no matter what we were doing and he would grab me just like the older boys grabbed all the girls.

I tried telling Margaret about what all the boys were doing to the girls, but she told me she didn't have time for stories. I decided to toughen up and use Prudence's advise from the foster care facility, don't take shit from anyone. I was done being victimized.

"You aren't going to take advantage of me anymore. Fuck off asshole," I told him.

"What did you just say to me bitch?" Adam said, back handing me across my face.

"Don't you ever touch me again!" I yelled.

"You aren't going to tell me what to do," Adam said, grabbing me by my hair and throwing me on my bed.

I tried to fight him off, kicking and screaming as loud as I could, but he was physically stronger than I was. He managed to get both of my hands above my head and hold them with only one of his hands. With his other hand he managed to finagle both his pants and mine before taking advantage of me.

After Margaret's reaction when I told her about the inappropriate touching, I knew I couldn't tell her about this. She would probably call me a liar and I would face worse abuse from Adam if he knew I had told anyway.

After a week of the same thing everyday, I was so happy when Janet Russell and Leigh came to visit me on the same day. I felt as though I could finally be saved.

"Well, first of all, did you talk to Margaret about what Adam and the boys are doing?" Janet asked.

"Of course I did. When she told me she didn't have time for my stories, I tried to make him stop on my own. That only made him more aggressive and I felt like I was not being heard," I told her.

"Are you trying to say this is her fault?" Leigh questioned Janet.

"Look, all I'm saying is that she seems to have a problem at every foster home she is assigned to. Maybe she should stop giving the males in the home the impression that she is willing to give them what they want," Janet said, shrugging her shoulders and looking me up and down.

"This is ridiculous. If you don't do something, I will. This is why most of the children living in the foster care system feel like they don't have a voice and are unable to get away from their abuser. Since you are completely incompetent to do your job, I will find her a home," Leigh said, grabbing my hand and leading me toward my room.

"I'm sorry detective, but you can't do that. I have been assigned to her. She is my case," Janet said from behind us.

"The hell I can't. My job description says I'm over you. If you don't fix this, I will have you removed as a social worker. Besides, she is not a case, she's a person," Leigh told her, before continuing to my room with me.

"What's going to happen now?" I asked her, as we entered the dorm.

"I have a list of foster homes that I have personally investigated and we will try each one until you find one that you are comfortable in," she told me.

"I want to find Jojo. We had a real connection and he was taken from here and adopted about a month ago. I want to go live with him."

"I'm sorry sweetie, I'm not able to do that. The couple that adopted him only adopts children who have police records and are on the wrong path in life. They feel as though they can change them and turn them into successful adults."

"What was he arrested for? We never talked about it because it was never important."

"Petty theft and a runaway."

"Damn it. Why can't the family I choose, just stay with me. Is this going to happen every time?"

"No sweetie. One day you will find a family that will stay with you forever."

"Well, let's get the fuck out of here," I said, slinging my bag over my shoulder.

Twenty Four

For the next two and a half years I bounced around through thirteen different foster homes. I had hope that one day I would end up in the same home with Jojo. I did everything I could to get kicked out of each home.

I beat the shit out of one girl at one home and pretended to have night terrors in another home. I spent the first few days figuring out what would drive the foster family to kick me out and that's how I got out of each one, although there were a few that, after a week of driving them crazy, I just flat out ran away from.

At the Butler home, I snuck out the window after everyone went to sleep. I didn't think it was fair that the couple forced their six foster children to work in their store after school everyday. I was thirteen and the youngest in the house. I was also the only one in the house who hated working and being told what to do. I vowed to own my own business when I grew up, so I wouldn't be told what to do. I wanted to be the one to tell other people what to do.

One night after we all arrived home, I went straight to the room I was staying in and packed my bag. Once everyone was in bed for the night, I waited exactly two hours before climbing out the open window in the bedroom and taking off down the street.

It took me a couple of days to walk to Leigh's house. She was always happy I was uninjured, but always disappointed I had left another foster home.

At the Danzig home, I walked right out the front door, in the middle of the day, while everyone else watched television. I had just turned fourteen and they insisted that the children in their home pull their own weight. Each child was to find a way to make their own money and purchase everything themselves.

Each Sunday we were all taken to the grocery store with a personal budget and we would each buy our own groceries, which were kept in our own personal refrigerator and cabinet in their garage. After two weeks of living in their home, I had failed to find a source of income, to which Mr. Danzig informed me that I would no longer be eating for free.

I packed my bag one Saturday afternoon while everyone else was gathered in the living room and walked right out the front, slamming the door behind me. The Danzig couple followed me out and wanted to know where I was going. Without turning around, or speaking, I kept walking down the street and just raised my hands to my shoulders with my middle fingers pointing up.

That time, it took me a little longer than a couple of days to get to Leigh's house because I didn't want to see the disappointment in her eyes. I stayed a little longer out on the streets only to prolong the inevitability of ending up at another foster home.

The next one was the Johnson home. They had a large family of fifteen kids and they enjoyed having all of their kids around, so when one of their kids grew up and moved out, they replaced them with a foster child. A couple of months in a crowded home and I was done.

One morning I left to go to school with the other kids, but I never went inside. I just walked right passed the school and only spent one night on the street before Leigh picked me up. I was alone that night, but I was relieved to have time to myself along with peace and quiet.

When I was just shy of my fifteenth birthday, I was taken to the Thompson home. The couple tried hard to connect with me, but I would just use profanity toward them, in front of the younger kids. One day they decided they could no longer keep me in the house, so I packed my bags when I heard them calling social services to come get me. A social worker showed up the next day.

Leigh's visits over the years became few and far between because her job became more demanding. As time went on, she began investigating crimes against children and it wasn't just happening to children in the foster care system. Although, she was the one I always went to when I ran away from the homes. It seemed as though the older I got, the less social services cared about where they placed me, but Leigh was concerned as to what would happen to me once I turned eighteen.

A couple of months after I had turned fifteen, Leigh was taking me to a home, that she hoped, was my last. I just wanted to feel the same connection with someone that I had with both Johnny and Jojo.

"You only have three years left before you age out of the system. Now is the time to choose family over loneliness. If you don't embrace the family life, you will end up living on the streets the day you turn eighteen," she told me.

"Well, at least I know I can take care of myself on the streets. I've done it several times," I said.

"Mackenzie, do you want to be one of the kids that lived through the foster care system, but just turned into a burden on society, rather than the one who turned a horrible situation into a happy ending?"

"I don't give a shit what happens to me now. Fuck this, I just want to hurry up and be eighteen and be out on my own so I don't have to keep moving around."

"I hope this is your last home. You need to accept it."

"It is my twentieth foster home, so I hope it is too," I told Leigh, sighing heavily.

"You will be happy to know that there are only two other girls that live there. The foster parents are very strict and won't give up on you. They do, however, have high expectations on academics. If you want to be rewarded, you must excel," Leigh informed me.

"Well, I guess it's time to give up on the idea that I will ever see Jojo again. I might as well accept the shitshow that has become my life and just go with it. Hopefully the girls aren't stuck up bitches and I can get along with them."

"Alright Mackenzie, that's enough with the profanity. I will do what I can to visit you at least once a month to check on you, but I can't guarantee it. Please, just make it work."

"I will stay there until I age out of the system, then we can figure out where I go from there," I said, as Leigh pulled up to the house.

I was grateful it was a large two story home. That way I would always be able to get away from everyone if I needed to. The home looked newer and the lawn appeared as though it was still growing. The one tree in the front lawn was being guided with T-bar and wire.

As we exited the vehicle, I reached into the back seat and grabbed my bag. We stepped up to the front door and Leigh knocked. When the door was opened, a woman in her late thirties, with long blonde hair, dressed in a one piece pant suit stood on the other side.

"You must be Mackenzie. Please, come in," the woman said, moving to the side, so we could enter the house.

While Leigh talked with the lady of the house, I was shown to a room by the two other girls. We each got our own rooms, which I was ecstatic about.

"Well Mackenzie, I'm Charlotte and this here is Jillian. Jillian was adopted as a baby and I came to stay here when I was little. The Mrs. is kind of a bitch some times, but as long as you get good grades and follow the rules, she can be tolerable," Charlotte said, laughing.

"Charlotte, why is your language always so colorful? Don't you ever have anything nice to say?" Jillian said.

"Don't listen to her. Mom and dad like her best and she has been here the longest, so she doesn't know what it's like to bounce around from home to home," Charlotte said.

"Well, Charlotte came here and figured out how to manipulate them into believing she's a good person. So they allowed her to stay as a long term foster child without being adopted," Jillian said, over her shoulder as she looked out the window.

"Jillian is just bitter because she actually is a good person and doesn't have a bad bone in her body," Charlotte said, walking up behind Jillian and placing her hands on Jillian's hips.

"I'm not bitter, I'm proper," Jillian stated, pushing Charlotte's hands off her and walking over to the bed.

Both Jillian and I sat down on the bed as Charlotte leaned against the window sill. Jillian's hair color was the same as the foster mom, but looking at her roots proved it was bleached, her roots were almost black. Charlotte's hair was dark, curly and unkempt. It was apparent that the foster parents had no idea how to deal with her hair.

As the months went on, it became evident I was being treated like the black sheep by the foster parents, but Charlotte and Jillian accepted me as family and we became close. Charlotte taught me how to manipulate the bitch into being nicer to me, but some days I just couldn't get along with that blonde bimbo.

During family fun nights, the foster parents told me I had to stay in my room. The foster dad in the house was a total tool and he knew my history. It didn't matter what kind of manipulation technique I tried to use from Charlotte, he just did not like me. Even though I was excluded from family functions with my foster parents, Charlotte and Jillian made my time at the house bearable.

Leigh came to see me whenever she could, but I was enthralled with spending time with my new foster sisters, so it didn't bother me. One day when I was at school, I was called to the front office to speak with Leigh. At that time, I was seventeen and hadn't seen her for quite a few months. I was so glad she had come to visit again. I didn't understand why she had come to the school instead of the house, but I wasn't going to question it.

"Hey Mackenzie. How are you doing?" Leigh asked, hugging me.

"Charlotte and Jillian are great. The three of us are going to get our own home after graduation," I told her.

"That's wonderful. I'm so glad you have found your family."

"Speaking of family, were you ever able to find my mother?"

"No sweetie. Unfortunately, we feel she has changed what she looks like from the description that the front desk clerk from the hotel gave us. We also think she may have left town. I'm so sorry."

"It's okay now. I don't need her. I have you and now I have Charlotte and Jillian. You don't have to continue looking for her. It has been eleven years and I have moved on."

"Are you sure? You know it could still be possible that we could find her," Leigh said.

"No, she didn't want me, so I don't want her. I'm going to live my life without worrying that she could pop back up," I told her, relieved.

Twenty Five

After Leigh left my school that day, it was the last time I saw her. A social worker still came by once a month to talk to me and see how I was doing. I never learned their names because since Leigh was able to get Janet Russell fired for being unsympathetic toward the protection of the children, there was usually someone new every time. Sometimes I would see a social worker twice, but never in a row.

"Mackenzie, are you ready for graduation?" the social worker asked.

"Hell yeah I am. I can't wait to start my life outside of the foster care system. It's going to be great not to have these monthly visits with someone who sits across from me and pretends to care," I told her, tilting my head and raising my eyebrows.

"Well, I can always put in my report that you are safe and don't need another visit until your last. That way we won't see you again until you turn eighteen and we release your foster care file to you."

"That's only in a couple months. I don't care what you put in your file. Are we done here? I have to go to work."

"Okay, we are done. I will be sure to be the one to visit you on your eighteenth birthday."

"Good for you. See you in a couple of months," I said, running up the stairs to change for work.

The couple of months leading up to my eighteenth birthday, I could only hope that my foster parents wouldn't kick me out of the house. I would turn eighteen a month before we would graduate from high school and with the hatred my foster parents showed me, I couldn't be guaranteed a home for the last month.

"There's no way they would be that shitty," Charlotte told me.

"I wouldn't put it past them. They never really wanted me here in the first place," I said.

"Don't worry Mackenzie, we will make sure that you are able to stay here with us until the three of us can move out together," Jillian informed.

After graduation, Charlotte, Jillian and I were planning to take a trip out of the country. That was our way to start our own lives and be free of the foster care system.

Our foster parents allowed us to get jobs when we turned sixteen, so we could save up for our European trip. Any allowance we received, for doing our chores around the house, also went into our trip fund. It took us up to our graduation to make sure we had enough money for a full month trip.

We went to Europe for the month. One day, we had entered a café in London and Charlotte spotted a young guy across the cafe and pointed him out.

"That's the man I'm going to marry" Charlotte said.

"Charlotte, you don't even know him. He could be one of those crazy European guys who kidnap female tourists and sell them into prostitution," I warned her.

"Oh Mackenzie, you worry too much," Charlotte said, batting her eyelashes at him from across the room.

"Don't you ever watch 20/20? Barbara Walters reports all the time about American women who travel to Europe and are never seen again. If they are found, they are part of some kind of perverted old man sex slave group," I informed.

"I haven't even talked to him yet. Can I at least meet him before you label him as a perverted old man sex slave group leader?" she said, giggling.

"Fine, but if he asks you to come back to his hotel room with him, we're leaving and you're coming with us," I told her, wagging my finger in her face.

Fortunately, he was American. He was also on a graduation trip to Europe and he lived in the same state. As soon as the three of us got home, Charlotte made plans with Tom Moore and they where married within a year.

I resented him for a while for taking away one of my best friends and my sister, but eventually, I accepted him as family as well.

Jillian and I decided to purchase a house together, but in the back of my mind, I was worried that she would leave me one day as well to get married. Eventually, it happened. She found Mark Geary and they were married within ten months.

She moved out of the house we shared and moved in with Mark. I didn't realize how badly I would feel abandoned once my foster sisters each found someone and I was left to suffer in silence.

Charlotte decided I was turning into an agoraphobic, since all I ever did was go to work and come home, so she made plans for us to have lunch every Wednesday; just the three of us. Then, Friday nights were reserved for me to be their fifth wheel at dinner.

C. L. Conolly is the author of the *Affair Series* starting with *Forbidden Affair.* As well as the stand alone title, *Friendly Misfortunes.* She has been writing stories since the age of six and after graduating high school, she then went on to gain an MFA in Creative Writing.

She has studied the sadistic minds of the most infamous serial killers as well as police and crime scene procedures in order to write accurately.

C. L. Conolly enjoys writing each first draft long hand by putting pen to paper. When she is not writing, she enjoys reading, running and spending time at home with her son, husband and dogs.

Facebook: C. L. Conolly - Author
Twitter: @CLConolly
Instagram: clconolly
Website: clconolly.com
YouTube: C. L. Conolly

KILLER
WORDS
PUBLISHING